INHERITED
BY HER ENEMY

INHERITED BY HER ENEMY

BY

SARA CRAVEN

First published in Great Britain 2015
by Mills & Boon, an imprint of Harlequin (UK) Limited,
Large Print edition 2015
Eton House, 18-24 Paradise Road,
Richmond, Surrey, TW9 1S⌐

© 2015 Sara Craven

ISBN: 978-0-263-25632-1

C460168284

Harlequin (UK) Limited's policy is to use papers that are natural, renewable and recyclable products and made from wood grown in sustainable forests. The logging and manufacturing processes conform to the legal environmental regulations of the country of origin.

Printed and bound in Great Britain
by CPI Antony Rowe, Chippenham, Wiltshire

To Eve, with love and thanks.

CHAPTER ONE

GINNY MASON SENT a wave and grateful smile to the last of the departing well-wishers, then closed the heavy front door against the raw chill of the late January afternoon with a deep sigh of relief.

That, she thought wryly, leaning a shoulder against the doorframe as she listened to the car draw away, was the worst part of the day over. At least she hoped so.

The crematorium chapel had been full, because her stepfather Andrew Charlton was popular in the locality and well respected as an employer too, being the recently retired head of his own successful light engineering company. But only a handful of those present had accepted Rosina Charlton's invitation to return to the house for the lavish buffet she'd arranged and few had stayed for very long.

They still think of us as interlopers, Ginny told herself, pulling a face, and they probably feel that Andrew should have been buried next to his first wife after a church service.

Or, maybe, word of Mother's plans has probably got around. Today Rosina had been the wistful, gracious chatelaine, fragile in black. Last night she'd declared peevishly that she couldn't wait to sell Barrowdean House and get away from all these stuffed shirts, to somewhere with a bit of life.

'The South of France, I think.' She nodded. 'One of those really pretty villas in the hills, with a pool. So nice for the grandchildren when they come to visit,' she'd added with an arch look at her younger daughter.

'For God's sake, Ma,' Lucilla had said impatiently. 'Jonathan and I have only just got engaged. We won't be thinking of a family for absolutely ages. I want some fun too.'

Nothing new there, then, Ginny had thought to herself. Although she supposed Cilla could hardly be blamed. She was 'the pretty one', whereas Ginny, as her mother often pointed out, took after her father. Her creamy skin and neat figure did not compensate for the fact that her hair was light brown instead of blonde, and her eyes were not blue but grey. And her face could best be described as unremarkable.

Cilla on the other hand was a true golden girl, spoiled since birth by everyone.

Even Andrew had not been immune, because, when she'd returned from completing her education at an expensive establishment in Switzerland, while he might have muttered about her doing some proper training and getting a job, he'd never insisted that she become gainfully employed.

And when she'd caught the eye of Sir Malcolm and Lady Welburn's only son, and courtship had proceeded rapidly to engagement, he'd nodded in a resigned way, as if weighing up the probable cost of the wedding.

An occasion he had not lived to see, thought Ginny, her throat tightening as she remembered the tall, thin kindly man who'd provided such safety and security in their lives for the past ten years.

As she began to recover from the immediate shock of Andrew's death, she was already wondering why they hadn't been warned about his heart condition.

But, as yet, she'd had no real opportunity to grieve. Her mother and Cilla's hysterical reaction to their loss had demanded all her time and attention to begin with, and then had come the bombshell of Rosina's decision to sell Barrowdean and move as soon as a buyer could be found, which had knocked her sideways all over again.

There was, her mother had claimed defiantly, nothing to keep her here, because Cilla, marrying darling Jonathan, would be well taken care of.

'While you have your job at that funny little café, Virginia,' she'd added. 'I'm sure someone in the village will have a room you can rent.'

It had been on the tip of Ginny's tongue to say that the café was no longer just a job, but a prospect for the future, and accommodation might not be an issue. However, on second thoughts, she decided to keep quiet.

She moved away from the door and stood, irresolute for a moment, listening to the murmur of voices and chink of china and cutlery from the dining room, where Andrew's elderly housekeeper Mrs Pelham, and Mavis from the village were clearing away the remains of the buffet.

Which we'll probably be eating for the rest of the week, she told herself ruefully.

Mrs Pel, of course, was another problem for her to worry about. Not that the old lady was under any illusions. She knew quite well that Rosina had been trying to get rid of her ever since she'd come to live at Barrowdean House, using Mrs Pel's age and growing infirmity as her excuse. But Andrew had ignored all hints.

Apart from his personal fondness for her, he said, Mrs Pelham was part of Barrowdean, and ran the house like clockwork. When she decided to retire, she would tell him. Until then, no change would be made.

Now, of course, there was no such curb, and the housekeeper's dismissal would be high on the list of Rosina's 'things to do'.

Ginny knew she ought to lend a hand with the clearing, as she did with most of the household chores these days, out of regard for Mrs Pel's arthritis, but instead she headed for Andrew's study to make sure everything was ready for the formal reading of the will.

'What a ridiculous performance,' Rosina had said scathingly. 'When we're the sole beneficiaries.'

I hope it's that simple, thought Ginny, aware of a brief and inexplicable pang of anxiety.

However, Mr Hargreaves, the solicitor who'd always handled Andrew's affairs had been quite adamant that in this, at least, his client's wishes should be observed, and had arranged to call at five o'clock.

The study had always been Ginny's favourite room, probably because the walls were lined with books, and she'd enjoyed curling up in a chair by the fire, silent and engrossed, while Andrew worked at his desk.

She hadn't been in here since his death, and she had to brace herself to open the door, hardly believing that he would not be there to look up and smile at her.

But there was still a living presence in the room. Barney, her stepfather's five-year-old Golden Labrador was stretched out on the rug in front of the fire.

As she entered, he raised his head, and his tail beat a brief tattoo on the rug, but he didn't jump up and come over to push his muzzle into her hand. That was a privilege still reserved solely for the beloved master who would not return.

'Poor old boy,' Ginny said softly. 'Did you think I'd forgotten you? I promise I'll take you out again once this will-reading business is sorted.'

Although Barney, of course, was another problem. Her mother who disliked dogs—the mess, the smell—was already talking about sending him to the vet to be put down, and Ginny felt sick at the prospect.

She would take him herself like a shot, but until

she knew for certain what her own prospects were, her hands were tied.

She added logs to the fire, switched on the lamps, made sure there were enough chairs, then walked across to draw the curtains over the French windows. As she did so, she saw the flash of car headlights approaching up the drive, and glanced at her watch, verifying that Mr Hargreaves, usually a stickler for punctuality, was in fact early.

Probably because this is undoubtedly going to be his least favourite appointment of the day, and he wants to get it over with, she thought, with a sigh.

When the doorbell rang a few minutes later, she was surprised to find Barney accompanying her across the hall, whimpering with excitement.

He must think Andrew's simply been away and has just returned, she told herself, her throat tightening again. But it's the sound of his key that he's always recognised in the past.

She tucked a hand into his collar, knowing that not everyone relished being hit amidships by a large and exuberant Labrador, and opened the door.

She began, 'Good evening,' then stopped with the words 'Mr Hargreaves' freezing on her lips.

Because the man standing in front of her was certainly not the family solicitor. For a moment, he seemed part of the darkness, his black trench coat hanging open over a charcoal grey suit, with a leather satchel on a long strap hanging from one shoulder. His hair was dark too, and glossy as a raven's wing, even if it was over-long and slightly dishevelled.

For the rest of him, he was tall, with a lean tanned face and heavy-lidded dark brown eyes. Not good-looking, was her overriding impression. Not with that thin-lipped, uncompromising mouth, nor that beak of a nose, which looked as if it had been broken at some point, and a chin that by contrast seemed to threaten to break any fist which dared approach it.

And yet he was, in some incomprehensible way, faintly familiar, and she found this disturbing.

But Barney had no reservations about the newcomer. With a whine of delight, he broke free of Ginny's suddenly slackened hold and pushed himself against the stranger's legs.

'Barney! Sit down, sir.' There was a faint quiver in her voice, but the dog obeyed, tail thumping and brown eyes gazing up in liquid adoration.

She said, 'I'm sorry. He's not usually like this with—people he doesn't know.' *Or with people he does know most of the time...*

The man bent and stroked the smooth golden head, gently pulling Barney's ears.

'It is not a problem.' A low-pitched voice, slightly husky, with a definite accent that was certainly not local.

As he straightened, Ginny realised she was being looked over in turn. His face betrayed nothing, but she sensed he was not impressed by what he saw.

Which makes two of us, she thought.

She took a breath. 'I'm sorry. Were we expecting you?'

'Mr Hargreaves expects me,' he said. 'He asked me to meet him here.'

'Oh—I see,' she said untruthfully, trying and failing to connect this tough who appeared to need a shave with the ultra-conservative firm of Hargreaves and Litton. 'In which case, you'd better come in.'

And if he turns out to be a master burglar and/ or a mass murderer, she addressed Barney silently, I shall blame you.

She turned and walked back to the study, knowing without looking round that he was following her, the dog at his side.

She said, 'If you'll wait here. Would you like some coffee?'

'Thank you, but no.'

Civil, she thought, but terse. And the way he was looking round him, appraising what he saw, much as he'd done with herself, made her even more uneasy.

'Mr Hargreaves should be here at any minute,' she went on, and he responded with a silent inclination of the head, as he put down his satchel and shrugged off his trench coat. His shirt she noticed was pearl-grey, open at the neck and he wore a black tie tugged negligently loose.

Feeling she was observing altogether too much, Ginny murmured something about her mother and sister and retired.

In the drawing room, Rosina rose, smoothing her skirt. 'I presume Mr Hargreaves has arrived, and we can get this farce over and done with.'

'No, that was someone else—from his office apparently,' said Ginny, frowning a little as she remembered the tanned and calloused fingers that had fondled Barney. Not, she thought, the hand of someone who worked at a desk. So, who on earth…

Her train of thought was interrupted as the doorbell sounded yet again. She rose but was halted by her mother.

'Stay here, Virginia. It's Mrs Pelham's job to answer the door, while she remains under this roof,' she added ominously.

Just as if she didn't know how many of the household tasks Ginny had quietly taken over in the past six months.

The drawing room door opened again to admit Mrs Pelham, back upright, but walking with the aid of a stick. 'Mr Hargreaves is here, madam. I have shown him into the study.'

Rosina nodded. 'I'll join him presently.'

She and Cilla disappeared upstairs to tidy their hair and no doubt freshen their make-up. Ginny, content that she looked neat and tidy enough in her grey skirt and cream polo-necked sweater, remembered the unexpected arrival and grabbed an extra chair on her way through the hall.

As she entered the study, she saw him deep in quiet conversation with Mr Hargreaves, who immediately broke off to come across and relieve her of her burden.

His normally calm face was creased in worry. He said quietly, 'I am so sorry for your loss, Miss Mason. I know how close you were to your step-father. Even now, it hardly seems possible...' He paused, patted her arm and went back to the desk, placing the chair beside his own.

Then there was the sound of voices and Rosina and Cilla entered, their blonde hair in shining contrast to their black dresses.

Mr Hargreaves's unknown companion glanced round and paused, his attention totally arrested by the exquisitely melancholy vision being presented, particularly by Cilla, who was even carrying a handkerchief, and whose dress clung to every delectable contour of her exquisite figure.

Don't even think about it, Ginny advised him under her breath. Cilla prefers the smooth, safe type. You don't qualify on either count.

Rosina paused. 'What is that dog doing in here? Virginia, you know quite well that he should be in the kitchen quarters. Must I do everything myself?'

The stranger spoke. 'Why not a compromise?' He snapped his fingers, and Barney got up from the rug and ambled across to curl up under the desk, out of sight.

Which was not a thing a country solicitor's clerk should do in front of his boss, thought Ginny, startled. And that was definitely a foreign accent. So who was he?

As Rosina began an indignant, 'Well, really,' she took her mother's hand, giving it a warning squeeze and led her to the big chair by the fireplace, herself perching on its arm, hoping that her sixth sense, so often a warning of trouble ahead, was wrong in this instance.

Mr Hargreaves began in the conventional manner, dealing first with the small bequests, to the gardener, and various charities. There was also a generous pension for Margaret Jane Pelham 'in recognition of her years of devoted service', and the use of one of the village properties Andrew owned for the whole of her lifetime.

She should have been here to hear that for herself, Ginny thought wearily, but her mother had vetoed the idea.

'Now we come to the major provisions in the will,' Mr Hargreaves continued, and Rosina sat up expectantly.

'For my wife, Rosina Elaine Charlton,' he went on. 'I direct that she receive an annuity of forty thousand pounds, payable on the first of January each year, and the use of Keeper's Cottage during her lifetime, its repair and maintenance to be paid from my estate.'

'An annuity—a cottage?' Rosina, her voice shaking, was on her feet. 'What are you talking about? There must be some mistake.'

'Mother.' Ginny guided her back into her chair, aware that she too was trembling. 'Let Mr Hargreaves finish.'

'Thank you, Miss Mason.' He cleared his throat, awkwardly. 'There is one final and major item.' He paused. 'All other monies and property of which I die possessed, including Barrowdean House and my shares in Charlton Engineering, I bequeath to my natural son, Andre Duchard of Terauze, France.'

There was an appalled silence. Ginny stared at the man sitting beside the solicitor, his dark face expressionless. Andre, she thought. The French version of Andrew. And, while she'd been aware of some faint familiarity, Barney—Barney had known in some unfathomable way. Barney had recognised him as family.

Then: 'Natural son?' Rosina repeated, her voice rising. 'Are you telling me that Andrew has left everything—*everything*—to some—some bastard? Some Frenchman none of us have heard of until now?'

'But I, *madame*, have heard a great deal about

you,' Andre Duchard said silkily. 'I am enchanted to make your acquaintance at last.'

'Enchanted?' Rosina gave a harsh laugh. 'Enchanted to think that you've robbed me of my inheritance, no doubt. Well, don't count your chickens. Because I intend to fight this outrage if it takes everything I've got.'

Which at the moment, thought Ginny, is forty thousand a year and the use of a cottage. Damn all else. As for me—well, I can't think about that now. The priority is damage limitation.

She put an arm round her mother's shoulders. She said quietly, 'I'm sorry, Mr Hargreaves, but I think we're all in a state of shock. As my mother says, we hadn't the least idea that Monsieur Duchard existed. But I imagine Andrew arranged for his heir's credentials to be thoroughly checked.'

Mr Hargreaves took off his glasses and wiped them carefully. He said, 'Indeed, yes. Mr Charlton always knew he had a son, and obtained legal recognition of his paternity according to French law. He also has letters and photographs going back to the time the boy was born, which my father kept for him in a box at our offices.' He paused again. 'This was a matter of discretion as Mrs Josephine

Charlton was still alive at that time, and our client was anxious not to distress her.'

'And what about my feelings?' Rosina demanded tearfully. 'He wasn't so caring about them. Ten years of devotion rewarded by a pittance and the use of a hovel!'

Ginny groaned under her breath, stingingly aware of Andre Duchard's sardonic smile, as he absorbed every word and gesture, then froze as he looked directly at her, the dark brows drawing together as if he'd been presented with a puzzle he had yet to master.

Hastily, she averted her gaze.

'Mother, why don't you come upstairs and lie down,' she suggested gently. 'I'll ask Mrs Pelham to make you some tea and...'

'I want nothing from that woman. Don't you realise Andrew has treated me the same as her—a servant—in this disgusting will? Oh, how could he do such a thing? He must have been quite mad.'

Her eyes suddenly sharpened. 'But of course, that's it. Something must have disturbed the balance of his mind. Isn't that what they say?'

'I think you are referring to suicide, *madame,*' Andre Duchard corrected gently.

'Well, whatever.' Mrs Charlton waved a dismissive hand. 'We can still have the will overturned. You hear about such things all the time.'

'I strongly advise against any such action,' Robert Hargreaves said gravely. 'You have no case, Mrs Charlton. Your husband was a sane and rational man, who wished to openly recognise his son born outside wedlock. The will I have just read was drawn up two years ago.'

'But if this man is really Andrew's son, why is he called—Duchard or whatever it was? It sounds bogus to me.'

The Frenchman spoke. 'Duchard, *madame,* is the family name of my stepfather, who adopted me when he married my mother. I hope that sets your mind at rest,' he added silkily.

Seeing that Rosina's face had reddened alarmingly, Mr Hargreaves intervened. 'I suggest you take Virginia's advice, Mrs Charlton, and rest for a while. We will speak again in a day or two, when you're feeling calmer. There are other important matters that need to be discussed.'

'You mean I still have a bedroom in this house?' Rosina glared at both men. 'Your client isn't proposing to move in here and now?'

'I would not put you to such trouble, *madame.*' There was a thinly veiled note of amusement in

Andre Duchard's cool tones. 'I have a reservation at the hotel in the village, while I too have discussions with Monsieur Hargreaves.'

'May I offer you a lift, *monsieur*?' Robert Hargreaves was thrusting documents back into his briefcase, his relief palpable. 'I see you dismissed your taxi.'

'*Merci.* But with the flight and the journey here, I have been sitting too much. I think I will walk.' He put on his trench coat and swung the leather bag on to his shoulder.

As they turned to leave, Barney emerged from the desk and stood watching their departure, ears flattened and tail drooping, as if he felt he'd been deserted a second time.

It was a sentiment that Ginny had her own reasons to share. But she made herself accompany the two men to the front door and wish them a polite 'Good evening,' adding haltingly, 'I hope you understand my mother is very upset.'

'Of course,' Mr Hargreaves agreed reluctantly. 'I will postpone any further meetings with her until next week. Goodbye, my dear. I'm sure things will seem different in the morning.'

She smiled and nodded, reflecting bitterly that there was a very long evening to get through first.

'*Au revoir,* Virginie.' The drawled French version of her name made it sound softer, giving it an almost sensual intonation, she realised with sudden embarrassment. Not that he had any right to use it. She felt her face warm and had to restrain herself from taking a step back, in order to put extra distance between them. '*Et à bientôt,*' he added.

And this time the note of mockery was unmistakable, as he must know he was the last person she would ever wish to see again, soon or late.

She murmured something evasive, and shut the door, recalling how earlier she'd thought the worst was over.

With a sigh, she took herself off to the kitchen, to find Mrs Pelham sitting at the large scrubbed table reading a letter.

She said, 'Don't disturb yourself, Mrs Pel. I've come to make some tea. I'm afraid we've all had rather a shock.' She paused. 'It seems Mr Charlton has an illegitimate son—a Frenchman called Andre Duchard—and made him his sole heir.'

As she watched the housekeeper slowly remove her glasses and return them to their case, she added, 'But perhaps you knew that already.'

'No, Miss Ginny. But I knew there was something up earlier, Mrs Charlton having a carrying sort of voice, and Mavis all ears.' She was silent for a moment. 'So this French gentleman gets everything. Well, well.'

'However, it doesn't affect you,' Ginny hastened to assure her. 'Mr Charlton has made sure you'll be taken care of.'

'Now that I did know,' Mrs Pelham said calmly. 'He sat me down and talked it over with me two months since, and when Mr Hargreaves arrived, he gave me this letter with it all set out.' She added with sudden fierceness, 'He was a good man, the master, and I'll never say otherwise, even if he didn't always find the happiness he deserved.'

Ginny filled the kettle and set it on the big gas range. She said quietly, 'Mrs Pel—have you any idea who Mr Duchard's mother might have been?'

'I can't be certain, Miss Ginny.' The housekeeper rose stiffly and began to assemble cups and saucers on a tray. 'But I remember Linnet Farrell, the late Mrs Charlton's companion. Here for a year she was, then one day she was gone, to nurse her sick mother it was said. Except she'd told me once that her parents were dead.'

Ginny retrieved the milk from the fridge and filled a jug. 'What was she like?'

'Not much in the way of looks,' said Mrs Pelham.

'But there was a sweetness about her just the same, and she made the house a brighter place. And Mrs Josie took to her too, for a wonder.'

Ginny said slowly, 'I gather she was an invalid.'

'Nerves,' said Mrs Pelham. 'And disappointment. That's what it was at the start. She wanted a baby, you see, and it didn't happen. Three miscarriages, all at four months, in as many years, and the doctors warning her she'd never carry a child full-term. She got into one of those depressions. Ended up in a nursing home, more than once.'

She sighed, 'And when she was back at home, she spent all her time in bed, or lying on a couch. And poor Mr Charlton having to sleep in another room, as well.'

She lowered her voice. 'I'm sure she loved him, but I don't think she was very keen on married life, as it were. Not unless there was going to be a baby to make it worthwhile. But a man wouldn't see it like that.'

No.' Ginny emptied sugar into a bowl. 'I—I don't suppose he would.'

'And suddenly there was this kind, warm-hearted girl living in the house, and he was an attractive man when he was younger. Not that I ever saw anything untoward, mind you,' she added hastily.

'And Linnet was good for Mrs Josie. Got her out and about, driving her car, and even doing some gardening.

'But one day she just upped and left. Came in the kitchen to say goodbye, and it was plain she'd been crying.' She sighed again. 'And later on, Mrs Josie really did become ill, poor soul, with Parkinson's disease, and Mr Charlton was as good to her as any husband could be, and enough said.'

She nodded with a kind of finality then glanced at the Aga. 'And that kettle's boiling, Miss Ginny.'

Ginny's mind was whirling as she carried the tray into the study, but the torrent of grievance which greeted her soon brought her back to earth.

'Well, at least you've got this annuity thing, Mother,' Cilla was saying furiously. 'Whereas he didn't leave me a penny, the old skinflint.'

Ginny put the tray on the desk. She said mildly, 'Perhaps he thought it was unnecessary, as you're marrying into one of the richest families in the county.'

Cilla turned on her. 'And you're getting nothing too, so all that trying to wheedle your way into his good books was a waste of time. You're going to be worse off than any of us,' she added almost triumphantly.

'So it would seem,' Ginny agreed, sounding more cheerful than she felt, as she poured the tea. 'But please don't worry about it.'

'I'm not,' her sister said sulkily. 'I just want to know how we're going to pay for my wedding. Mother, you'll have to talk to Mr Hargreaves. Get some more money out of him somehow.'

As Ginny poured out the tea, she noticed something. 'Where's Barney?'

'I put him outside,' said her mother. 'I couldn't bear him in the room a moment longer,' she added, fanning herself with her handkerchief.

Ginny put down the pot. 'You do realise he might have wandered off?'

'What if he has? I told you I'm getting rid of him.'

'You can't do that,' Ginny flung over her shoulder as she headed for the door. 'Like everything else in this house, he probably belongs to Monsieur Duchard. And he's a valuable dog.'

She huddled on her quilted jacket, pulled on her Wellington boots and grabbed a leash and a torch from the shelf in the boot room before letting herself out through the back door. The temperature outside wasn't much above freezing, and she could see her breath like a cloud in front of her as she skirted the house, softly calling Barney's name, hoping he would be waiting anxiously on the terrace for readmission.

But there was no sign of him. Biting her lip, she went round to the side gate, left carelessly open, probably by the departing Mavis, and stepped out on to the lane leading to the common.

As she walked, she called again, sweeping the area with her torch, knowing that he could be anywhere. As she reached the edge of the common, she took a deep breath then gave three soft whistles as Andrew used to do.

In the distance, there was an answering bark and a moment later, Barney came loping into view, tail wagging and tongue hanging out.

'Good boy,' Ginny said, sighing with relief as she attached the leash to his collar, but as she turned back towards the house, he resisted, standing stock still, staring back the way he'd come, and whimpering softly and excitedly.

As if, she thought, he was waiting for someone. She raised the torch, aiming the beam across the scrubby grass and clumps of gorse. She said sharply, 'Who's there?'

But there was no reply or sign of movement, and

after a moment or two, Barney came out of alert mode and turned obediently for home.

You, my girl, she told herself grimly, had better stop being over-imaginative and get down to practicalities—like where you'll go, and how the hell you'll earn your living.

And, as she trudged back to the house, she found herself wishing, with a kind of bitter despair, that she'd never heard the name of Andre Duchard. Or, better still, that he'd never been born.

CHAPTER TWO

WHEN GINNY GOT back to the house, she found her
mother alone in the drawing room.

She said, 'Where's Cilla?'

'Off to the Manor to consult Jonathan about this
appalling situation.'

'In what way—consult?'

'How we can fight this fraudulent will, of course,'
said Rosina, the ominous throb returning to her
voice. 'Oh, I can hardly bear to think of Andrew—
his deceit—his betrayal of me. Of our love.'

She shook her head. 'To have had a son—in secret—all these years, and said nothing to me—his
wife. It beggars belief. It makes me almost wish...'

She broke off abruptly. 'Get me a brandy, Virginia. A large one. I need something to settle my
nerves.'

As Ginny busied herself with the decanter on a
side table, Rosina added abruptly, 'You're so fortunate not to suffer in this way. Cilla and I are so
sensitive, but nothing ever seems to affect you.'

'That's not true,' Ginny said quietly, as she brought her mother the brandy. 'But I don't see any mileage in fussing over things I can't change.'

'But if we all stand together...'

'We could end up looking grasping and silly.'

'You might change your tune if you were the one faced with penury.'

If only you knew, Ginny thought bitterly. Aloud, she said mildly, 'It's hardly that, Mother. Whole families have to manage on much less.' She paused. 'Why don't we go over tomorrow and have a look at the cottage? It may not be as bad as you think.'

Rosina tossed her head. 'You go, if you want. I refuse to set foot in the place.' She produced a handkerchief. 'Oh, Andrew, how could you do this to me?'

To which, presumably, no answer was expected. Ginny waited until Rosina had drunk some of her brandy, then suggested they should watch some television, figuring correctly that she would again be accused of being without feelings.

All the same, her mother allowed herself to be persuaded, and was soon deep in a drama series she enjoyed, leaving Ginny to pursue her own un-happy train of thought.

The Meadowford Café was the official name of

her present place of employment, but it had never been known in the village as anything but 'Miss Finn's'.

The original Miss Finn had been a cook in some very exclusive households before deciding to open her own establishment in an area where she'd spent several holidays and which she'd grown to love.

A round rosy lady, her phenomenally light hand with cakes and pastry had made the business a roaring success, opening for morning coffee, serving light lunches of homemade quiches, open sandwiches and interesting salads, and closing once afternoon teas had been served.

And when she eventually retired, her place was taken and her high standards maintained by her unmarried niece, Miss Emma Finn, also pink-cheeked and on the plump side and considered locally, with kindly affection, as another born spinster.

Ginny, her school days behind her, and with respectable exam results to treasure, had considered teaching as a career, but her mother had reacted in horror, protesting that Ginny was needed at home.

'Such an enormous house to run single-handed, and Mrs Pelham not really pulling her weight any more. And really, you *owe* it to Andrew.'

Eventually, Ginny had reluctantly agreed, only to find herself caught between her mother's steely resolve and Mrs Pel's stony resistance. After three largely unproductive months doing very little, she saw a card in Miss Finn's window asking for part-time assistance, applied and got the job.

'You're going to be a *waitress*?' Mrs Charlton had been appalled. 'But you can't possibly. Whatever will Andrew say?'

Which had turned out to be 'Good for you,' accompanied by a wink and a pat on the shoulder.

To Ginny's own surprise, she enjoyed working at Miss Finn's and it wasn't long before she joyously accepted Miss Emma's offer of full-time work.

Three years on, Ginny was still enjoying herself, while giving Mrs Pelham unobtrusive and now welcome support at home too.

However, a few months ago, Miss Emma had, to everyone's astonishment, announced her engagement, with the news that she would be moving to Brussels after her marriage.

So a quick decision about the future of the café was needed. The premises were leased from the Welburn estate, so all she needed was someone to buy the actual business, and she had offered first refusal to Ginny.

'I suppose it should be Iris Potter,' she'd confided anxiously, 'as she's been here the longest, but she does so rub people up the wrong way. And while you're young, Ginny, you're such a capable girl and the customers like you.'

It was, Ginny knew, a wonderful opportunity, but Miss Finn clearly had no idea of her financial position. Andrew, it was true, made her an allowance, which he'd increased once he realised just how much she did in the house, but, apart from her wages, that was it.

She'd gone to the bank with a business plan, but got nowhere. Too young, she was told, and with no collateral.

So, eventually, and reluctantly, she took her plan to Andrew, who had sat quietly and listened while she outlined her requirements and her proposed system of repayments.

'So,' he said, when she'd finished. 'You really want to become the new Miss Finn?'

'Well, yes,' she agreed, although that was not how she'd thought of it. 'It's a marvellous business, and since they built those two new housing estates over at Lang's Field we're nearly rushed off our feet.'

He held out his hand. 'Give me your paperwork,

my dear, and I'll look it over in detail and let you have my decision.'

But he was away a good deal over the three weeks that followed, and Ginny began to grow anxious, although the last thing she wanted to do was apply any pressure when he was at home.

Miss Emma, however, wanted an answer, and Ginny was just nerving herself to approach Andrew again when he himself broached the subject in the hall one night, just as she was going up to bed.

She heard him call her name and turned to find him standing at the foot of the stairs looking up at her, with his usual gentle smile. He said, 'Don't worry, my dear. I haven't forgotten about the new Miss Finn.'

But he did, thought Ginny, painfully. Because two days later he was dead, without, it seemed, leaving any instructions that would have secured her future. So, she was still—just a waitress, and on Monday she would have to tell Miss Emma that she was out of the running.

As the credits rolled on her mother's TV series, Mrs Charlton asked plaintively if there was to be any dinner that evening, or if Mrs Pelham was on strike.

'I told her we could manage for ourselves.' Ginny paused. 'There are plenty of cold cuts.'

Her mother pursed her lips. 'Funeral food. Is a warm meal too much to ask? Even an omelette would do.'

Grating cheese and whisking eggs in a basin, Ginny reflected ruefully how completely her mother had adapted to being a rich man's wife, and how hard she would find it to cope once more with her own cooking and cleaning.

She was just dividing the golden-brown fluffy omelette in two when she heard a door bang in the distance. And as she slid the two halves on to warmed plates and added grilled tomatoes, Cilla walked in.

'Is that supper? Thank God. I'm starving.' She grabbed both plates and a handful of cutlery and marched off, leaving Ginny gasping.

She buttered two thick slices from a crusty loaf, filled them generously with cold ham, and took her sandwich back to the drawing room where it was clear a tale of woe was in progress.

'I simply couldn't believe it,' Cilla was saying plaintively. 'I told them what had happened and how dreadful everything was, and they said nothing. Just looked at each other. Not a word of sympathy or concern.'

'Do you think they already knew?' Rosina asked, but Cilla shook her head.

'No, they were obviously surprised. Then Sir Malcolm said he supposed that Mr Duchard was staying at the Rose and Crown, and *she* said, "Of course, you'll call on him, my dear, and ask him to come to dinner."' She shook her head. 'When I heard that I was *stunned*. I waited for Jon to say something, to point out how upsetting that would be for us, but he never spoke. Just stared at the carpet.'

Ginny said quietly, 'You'll find, Cilla, that Jonathan generally agrees with his mother.'

Her sister turned to stare at her, sudden malice glinting in her blue eyes. 'Not always. If he did, you'd be engaged to him instead of me. I'm sure the Welburns had you down as the daughter-in-law of choice, so it was hard luck for all of you when I came back and Jonathan decided he preferred me.'

'Darling,' Mrs Charlton said reproachfully. 'That's not very kind.'

'Nor is it true,' Ginny said quietly. 'Jonathan and I had a few casual dates, nothing more.'

Cilla tossed her head. 'That's certainly not what

Hilary Godwin says. She's been telling people you were crazy about him.'

Ginny shrugged. 'Hilary dated him too for a while. Maybe she has her own agenda. But that's unimportant. So let's get down to brass tacks.' She drew a breath. 'I think we, not the Welburns, should be the ones inviting Andre Duchard to dinner.'

Her mother gasped. 'You must be quite mad. Do you want us to become the laughing stock of the neighbourhood?'

'On the contrary,' Ginny returned with energy. 'That's exactly what I'm trying to avoid. If we're to maintain any sort of credit locally, we have to accept what's happened with as good a grace as we can manage. Accept Andrew's chosen heir.'

She listened to the shocked silence, then nodded. 'So tomorrow, I'll leave a note for him at the Rose and Crown. Nothing formal, but not kitchen sups either. And we'll invite the Welburns too. Make it an extended family occasion, and hopefully score a few points.'

She turned to her mother. 'And we can't play ostrich about the future, so I'll also call at Mr Hargreaves's office and get the key to the cottage.

Have a preliminary look round and make a list of anything that needs to be done.'

'You're taking a lot upon yourself,' Rosina said sharply.

'Someone has to,' said Ginny. 'And now, if you'll both excuse me, I'll take my sandwich up to my room. It's been a hell of a day, and I have a letter to write.'

As she closed the door behind her, she heard Cilla say furiously, 'Well, really...'

She went first to Andrew's study to get a sheet of notepaper from his desk. The envelopes were at the back of the drawer, but as she reached for them, her fingers grasped something bulkier.

My God, she thought in self-derision, as she pulled it towards her. Is this the moment I find a new will and all our problems are solved?

But what she'd discovered, in fact, was a map of France's Burgundy region. And no need to wonder why it was here, hidden away.

She stared down at it for a long moment, fighting her curiosity with resentment. Telling herself it was of no interest to her where Andre Duchard came from, even as she opened the map and spread it on the desk.

And found Terauze, heavily circled in black,

jumping out at her. Saw too that the map itself was beginning to tear at the creases, evidence of heavy use. All those trips abroad, she thought, dismissed airily by her mother as 'more boring business'. As some of them must have been, because the company order books were always full.

She'd once asked Rosina, 'Hasn't Andrew ever asked you to go with him?'

Her mother had shrugged evasively. 'My dear child, it's just one meeting after another. He's far better on his own.'

And so, of course, was Rosina with her golf lessons, her bridge friends, and her ladies luncheon club in nearby Lanchester, Ginny had mused drily.

But, under the circumstances, Andrew probably preferred to keep his secret, and encouraged his wife to stay at home.

But surely he must have realised the devastating effect the eventual revelation would have? Ginny argued. Or didn't he care?

No, she thought, I don't believe that for a minute. Because he was a kind, dear man, and taking on a widow and her two daughters must have been quite an enterprise. So what changed?

With a sigh, she looked back at the map. Burgundy, she mused.

Producing wine and Dijon mustard, and also, apparently, Andre Duchard. But if he was indeed Linnet Farrell's son, as Mrs Pel thought, how had she fetched up there?

So many questions for which she would probably never find answers. And she would be better employed in trying to establish better relations.

And on that resolve, she put the map back in the drawer, took her paper and envelope and went up to her room.

There was no problem obtaining the key for Keeper's Cottage the following morning. Mr Hargreaves did not work on Saturday mornings, but Ginny telephoned him at home after breakfast and he promised, sounding positively relieved, that he would arrange for it to be waiting for her at his office.

And for once, she was allowed without protest the use of her mother's smart little Peugeot.

Keeper's Cottage was on the very edge of the Barrowdean estate, and approached by a narrow lane. Built in mellow red brick, it was the kind of dwelling a child might draw, with a central front door flanked by two square windows, three more windows on the upper floor and chimneys at each end of the slate roof.

She pushed open the wooden gate and went up the flagged path between the empty winter flower beds. It was a bleak, iron-grey day with the promise of snow in the air, and Ginny huddled her fleece around her in the biting wind.

The front door creaked as she unlocked it and went in. She stood for a moment in the narrow hall, looking up the straight flight of stairs ahead of her, and taking a deep exploratory breath but she could pick up no telltale hint of damp, under the mustiness of disuse.

The downstairs rooms weren't large, but they'd be pleasant enough when redecorated. And surely it wouldn't be unreasonable to ask for the windows to be double-glazed.

The kitchen, reached from the dining room, had an electric cooker, and wall cupboards with space under the counter top for a washing machine and refrigerator.

Upstairs, she found two bedrooms facing each other across the passage, and a bathroom, where a pale blue suite made the room seem even chillier. The only other upstairs room was so small that it could never aspire to be a bedroom. Even a baby's cot would swamp it.

Ginny closed the door on it, her heart sinking.

For someone with enthusiasm and energy to match, Keeper's Cottage had real potential, she thought. Rosina, however, would regard it as a sentence of banishment, and maybe she had a point.

Once again, she found herself pondering the state of a marriage she had always assumed was perfectly content. After all, people didn't have to live in each other's pockets to be happy—did they?

But what do I know about marriage—or love, for that matter, she asked herself derisively, remembering Cilla's jibes earlier.

She'd liked Jonathan. She could admit she'd known a frisson of excitement when he called her, but that was as far as it had gone. Cilla's golden, glowing return had made sure of that. And any inward pangs she'd suffered from his defection were probably injured pride.

If I'd cared, I'd have fought for him, she told herself. Anyway, it's all in the past now, and, come June, he'll be my brother-in-law.

But where and what I'll be, heaven only knows.

She turned back towards the stairs then froze, as from the ground floor came the unmistakable creak of the front door opening and closing.

Her first thought was that it couldn't be a burglar because there was nothing to steal but the cooker.

All the same, she reached into her bag for her mobile phone, only to remember it was on charge on her bedside table.

She crept to the top of the stairs and looked cautiously down into the hall.

And there leaning against the newel post, completely at his ease as he looked up at her, was Andre Duchard. He said softly, 'Virginie.'

Once again, the sound of it made her feel as ridiculously self-conscious as if he had run a finger over her skin. She said huskily, 'I don't remember giving you permission to use my name. And what are you doing here?'

His gaze was unwavering. 'Examining my inheritance,' he said and smiled. 'All my new possessions.'

'Is that what you were doing last night—hanging round on the common?'

He shrugged. 'I needed to clear my head a little.'

Ginny bit her lip. 'Does Mr Hargreaves know that you're here?'

'But of course.' The dark brows lifted. 'I explained to him that I had never visited a hovel and wished to see for myself what such a place was like. He understood perfectly and gave me a key, which, *naturellement,* I have not needed to use. Because you were here first.'

She stared down at him. 'Didn't he tell you that I might be?'

'No, why should that matter?'

She couldn't think of a reason apart from how empty the cottage was—and how isolated. And that she had never expected to find herself alone with him—anywhere.

It occurred to her that in some odd way he made the hall seem even more cramped. And that with his untidy hair and the stubble outlining his chin, he was even less prepossessing in broad daylight than he had been the previous evening. He was wearing a dark roll-neck sweater under a thick jacket reaching to mid-thigh, and his long legs were encased in denim and knee-length boots.

And the silence lengthening between them was beginning to feel inexplicably dangerous.

She said hurriedly, 'I—I'm sorry about the hovel remark. I'm afraid my mother was too distraught to think what she was saying yesterday.'

'But today all that has arranged itself, and she is reconciled to her new situation?' His tone bit. 'I wish I could believe it was true.'

He glanced around him. 'And how will she like her new home?'

The obvious reply was 'She won't.' But Ginny decided to temporise.

'Well, it's rather small, and it does need refurbishing. But I think, in time, it could be—charming.'

'*Tout de même,* she did not accompany you here to see for herself.'

'I don't think you understand what a shock this has been—for all of us.' She bit her lip. 'We didn't even know that my—that your father was ill.'

'Nor I,' he said quietly. 'It was a matter he chose to keep to himself.'

'Like so many others,' Ginny said before she could stop herself.

The dark face was cynical. 'Perhaps he realised that news of my existence would be unwelcome.'

She said defensively, 'My mother could hardly blame him for something that happened long before she met him. If she'd been warned what to expect, she might not have this—sense of betrayal.'

'She feels betrayed?' The firm mouth curled. 'How interesting that she should think so.'

She moved restively. 'Well, I didn't come here to argue the rights and wrongs of the situation. I'll go and leave you to your inspection.' She began to descend the stairs, then paused. 'I almost forgot. I have an invitation for you.'

'An invitation,' he repeated, as if the word was new to him.

'Yes—to have dinner with us. Tomorrow evening.' She saw the look of incredulity on his face, and wished she'd never thought of the idea, let alone mentioned it. But it was too late now, so she hurried on, 'I was going to leave it at the hotel, but as you're here...'

She continued her descent, fumbling in her bag for the envelope, missed her footing on the uncarpeted stairs and stumbled forward, to be caught and lifted to safety in arms like steel bands.

Momentarily, her face was pressed against his chest, her nose and mouth filled with the scent of clean wool, soap and the more alien aroma of warm male skin, before she was set, ruffled and breathless, on her feet.

'You should have more care, *mademoiselle*,' he told her coolly. 'You do not need another tragedy in your family.'

Ginny flushed. 'I—I'm not usually so clumsy.' She handed him the envelope. 'You don't have to decide immediately, of course.' She added quickly, 'And we won't be offended if you're too busy.'

'But naturally I shall accept,' he said silkily. 'I am most intrigued that your mother should offer this olive branch.' He paused. 'It does, of course, come from her?'

She said quickly, 'Oh, yes.' But the brief hesitation preceding it had been fatal.

Strong fingers captured her chin, forcing her face up to meet his gaze.

'To be a good liar requires practice, *ma mie,*' he said softly. 'Let us hope you are not obliged to be untruthful too often, as I doubt you will ever excel. But clearly your powers of persuasion with Maman are *formidable.*'

Ginny wrenched herself free and stepped back. 'If it's frankness you want, *monsieur,* may I ask if you ever shave?'

'*Bien sûr*—on occasion. Especially if I am going to be in bed with a woman. But I doubt I shall be so fortunate,' he added pensively. 'Your beautiful sister already has a lover, *hélas.*'

She felt jolted as if her heart had skipped not one beat but several.

She said quietly, 'My sister is engaged to be married, *monsieur.* She has a fiancé.'

'And a rich one, according to the talk in the bar last night.' He shrugged. 'What no one can decide is if the affair will end in marriage, or simply end when he decides he has paid enough for his pleasures.'

Ginny gasped, and her arm swung back, but before she could wipe the cynical mockery from his face, his hand had grasped her wrist.

'So,' he said. 'The polite little girl has spirit. And what else, I wonder?'

He jerked her forward, his other arm going round her, pulling her against him, and as her lips parted in furious protest, his mouth came down hard on hers.

CHAPTER THREE

SHE COULDN'T STRUGGLE, or cry out. She could scarcely breathe. He was holding her too closely, her hands trapped between their bodies. Nor could she resist the practised movement of his lips on hers, or the slow sensual exploration of his tongue as he invaded the innocence of her mouth, tasting her sweetness. Drinking from her. Draining her, as she swayed in his arms, her mind reeling from the shock of it. And yet in some incalculable way—not wanting it to stop...

Only to find herself just as suddenly released.

'Oh, God,' she choked when she could speak, caught between anger and something dangerously like disappointment. 'How *dare* you?' And, her voice rising, *'How bloody dare you?'*

'Sois tranquille.' He had the audacity to grin at her. 'It took courage, *sans doute,* but what experiment does not?' He paused. 'So, *ma douce,* do I still have that invitation to dinner, or have I offended too deeply?'

Ginny was in a cleft stick. The dinner party was being held at her insistence. How could she cancel it without involving herself in truly hideous explanations? And if she claimed he was unavailable, she had no guarantee he would not find some way of letting the truth be known.

She swallowed hard. 'The invitation stands.'

He said slowly, 'You surprise me. Your family must want something very badly.'

She walked past him to the front door, and paused. 'A truce,' she said. 'Is the most that's hoped for. So, we'll expect you at seven-thirty.'

His smile still lingered. 'I shall look forward to it. *À demain.*'

Her hair had been loosened in the encounter, and whipped around her face as she walked to the car. She slid into the driving seat and gripped the wheel, waiting for the fierce trembling inside her to subside a little before starting the engine. As she probed her throbbing mouth with the tip of her tongue, it occurred to her that she could still taste him and felt her body clench harshly in response.

Get a grip, she adjured herself tersely. You've been kissed and by someone who knows how. You tried to hit him. He taught you a lesson. That's all there is to it.

But it was a learning curve she could have well done without.

She drove off with exaggerated care until Keeper's Cottage was a long way behind her, then pulled into a lay-by just outside the village and sat there until she felt calmer and more focused.

You have a dinner party to prepare for, she told herself. Concentrate on that. Forget everything else.

She'd discussed a possible menu with Mrs Pelham that morning, and they'd settled on salmon mousse, followed by Beef Wellington with roasted vegetables, and ending with white grapes in champagne jelly, and some good cheese.

She had returned the key to Mr Hargreaves' office, and was just emerging from the speciality cheese shop in the High Street, when she saw Sir Malcolm and Lady Welburn leaving the Rose and Crown, and waved to them.

As she reached the opposite pavement, she said breathlessly, 'I'm so glad I've seen you. I know it's terribly short notice but my mother would be delighted if you'd come to supper tomorrow evening, with Jonathan if he's free, and meet Andrew's son and heir, Andre Duchard.'

'My dear Virginia, what a very nice idea.' Lady

Welburn's slight air of constraint fell away, and she smiled with her usual warmth. 'We were just inquiring for him at the hotel, but he's out.'

She lowered her voice. 'I confess I was a little worried by Lucilla's attitude yesterday evening, so I'm very glad that Rosina's decided to do absolutely the right thing. Such a difficult situation for everyone otherwise. Thank your mother and tell her we'll all be there.'

Ginny smiled back, well aware that Lady Welburn was under no illusion whose scheme it really was.

'She'll be so pleased.'

Two hours later, she returned to the house, laden with bags from the supermarket at Lanchester. In the hall, she met her mother.

'Hi, she said. 'I'll just unpack this stuff, then I'll tell you about the cottage.'

'No need,' Rosina said airily. 'Because I'm not moving there.'

Ginny put down her carriers. 'Then where are you planning to live?'

'I'm staying right here. It's the obvious solution.'

'To what problem exactly?'

Rosina waved an impatient hand. 'To the future of Barrowdean. This Duchard individual will go back to France soon. He doesn't belong here and he must know it. But—he owns this house and he needs someone to look after it in his absence. Hiring resident caretakers would cost him a fortune, so I continue to live here rent-free and, in return, I make sure Barrowdean flourishes. I'd say it was a no-brainer.'

'I would too, but my definition of "no-brainer" is rather different.' Ginny shook her head. 'How did you dream up this fantasy?'

'It's a matter of hard practicality,' Rosina said sharply. 'You seem to have forgotten Cilla's wedding. The marquee and the caterers have already been booked, and well over two hundred people will be coming.'

She nodded briskly. 'Maybe this dinner party scheme isn't as ludicrous as I thought. It will give us a chance to talk him round.'

'I'm glad you think so,' Ginny said drily. 'It's tomorrow night—and the Welburns are coming too.'

Rosina frowned. 'Well, hopefully, they'll get him to see reason, especially over the wedding.' She paused. 'You saw him, did you—the Duchard man? How did he seem when you issued the invitation?'

Dangerous, thought Ginny, as a shiver ran through her. Aloud, she said, 'Surprised.'

Her mother shrugged. 'Judging by his appearance, I wouldn't think many dinner parties come his way. I only hope he knows how to use a knife and fork properly.' She shuddered. 'I cannot imagine how Andrew, always so fastidious, ever became involved with some peasant woman.'

Ginny, about to correct her, thought better of it, being unable to guarantee how Rosina might use any information she could garner.

She picked up her carriers. 'I must see to this food.'

'Well, come back as soon as you've done so. There were a lot more letters of condolence in the post just now, and I find them so painful. Perhaps you'd reply on my behalf, and get them out of the way.'

'Maybe Cilla could help.'

Rosina sighed. 'Cilla is lying down with one of her headaches. She's so sensitive, poor darling, and this awful business has shaken her very badly.'

'This awful business' seems to have the right idea, Ginny thought bitterly as she went off to the kitchen. I'd like to shake her myself.

She threw herself into preparations for the dinner party, doing as much advance food preparation as possible, then cleaning silver, washing glasses, and giving her favourite tablecloth a crisp ironing.

By the time she took the tray with afternoon tea, egg and cress sandwiches and a Victoria sponge into the drawing room, Cilla had come downstairs and was sprawled in an armchair.

'Did you visit this cottage?' she asked, without turning her gaze from the old black and white movie she was watching. 'What's it like? How many bedrooms?'

'Two reasonably sized and one like a storage cupboard,' Ginny returned briefly as she set down the tray.

'Two?' Cilla sat up. 'Did you hear that, Mummy? How on earth are we going to manage?'

Rosina glanced up from her magazine with a catlike smile. 'We'll worry about that when it happens, darling. I'll have lemon with my tea, Virginia,' she added. 'I need to be careful about my weight.'

'Well, I'm never sharing a bedroom,' Cilla said sharply.

'Do you include Jonathan in that sweeping statement?' Ginny asked mildly, handing her mother her tea.

Cilla shrugged. 'Plenty of married couples have separate bedrooms. It's supposed to make it more exciting. Retain that air of mystery.' She giggled. 'And when you are available—it makes men so much more grateful.'

Ginny took her tea and a sandwich and headed for the door. 'I never knew you were such a romantic,' she said drily as she left.

She collected the pile of letters from the hall table and took them to the study where Barney was lying by the newly kindled fire. He looked up as she entered and tentatively thumped his tail on the carpet, clearly bewildered as to why he spent so much time in the kitchen quarters these days.

'You and me both, sweetie,' she told him as she sat down.

The letters were just as difficult to deal with as she'd suspected. They were imbued with grief for Andrew's death and warmth and gratitude for his life. She read about his generosity, his fairness, and his personal kindness, particularly to former members of his workforce.

And after the first half dozen or so, she put her head down on the desk and wept a little, wondering where this man had gone, and why he'd changed so much.

* * *

By Sunday evening, winter had returned inside and out, with brief snow showers adding to the general chill.

Because all Ginny's attempts to reason with her mother over the caretaker scheme had got nowhere.

'Then at least ask him privately,' she'd begged at last, but Rosina waved her away.

'No, it's a perfect opportunity,' she declared buoyantly. 'The Welburns are our nearest neighbours and he'll want to make a good impression.'

'Well, I don't believe Mr Duchard will give a damn about what the neighbours think of him,' Ginny returned wearily. 'His home is in France so he won't be around long enough to care.'

Her mother tutted impatiently. 'Really, Virginia. Can you please stop being so negative. It's very depressing.'

And being a widow isn't? Ginny thought bitterly.

Working companionably and efficiently with Mrs Pel to produce the meal itself lifted her spirits however, and if she could only have put on her 'Miss Finn' pinny and simply served the food without having to join the party round the table, she'd have been happier still.

For one thing, she had no idea what to wear.

Most of the clothes in her wardrobe were of the workaday variety, entirely through her own choice. After a day on her feet in the café, followed by the domestic demands of Barrowdean, she was glad of the excuse to avoid the local social whirl, such as it was.

Lady Welburn had the right idea, she thought wistfully, generally appearing in a series of long skirts in jewel-coloured velvet run up for her by the village dressmaker, and teaming them with plain black cashmere tops.

She, however, would have to wear the Dress. She took it from the wardrobe and pulled a face at it. Mid-calf-length, long-sleeved and high-necked in taupe jersey, it had been bought for the Christmas before last when she was running short of time and temper.

And she could say with total truth it did nothing for her at all, except fit where it touched.

Never mind, she told herself. The best thing you can be at this blighted party is insignificant. And no more bright ideas either. They have this way of coming back to bite you in the rear.

She showered, dried her hair into its usual smooth bob, put on the taupe dress and went downstairs, knowing that neither her mother nor Cilla would put in an appearance until the last minute.

She checked the fire in the drawing room, and the drinks tray, then went along to the kitchen to fetch the bowls of nibbles.

She pushed open the door, and halted, her throat tightening in shock. Because Andre Duchard was there, perched on the edge of the kitchen table—a thing Mrs Pel never permitted—helping himself from a packet of cashew nuts.

He was wearing the dark suit again, with a white shirt setting off the sombre magnificence of a grey silk tie. That mane of hair was still too long but had at least been combed into some kind of order and, as she saw instantly, her own face warming, he had shaved.

He looked her over in turn, his brows rising quizzically as if confirming her own opinion of her dress, then gave a polite inclination of the head. '*Bonsoir.*'

Withstanding a desire to grind her teeth, Ginny uprooted herself from the doorway and took a step forward. 'I—I didn't realise anyone was here yet.'

'I was unforgivably early.' He did not look or sound particularly repentant. 'But I wished an opportunity to speak with Marguerite who was a friend to my mother.' He smiled at her, and took another cashew. 'But you already know that, I think.'

Ginny said stiffly, 'Mrs Pelham believed she knew her identity, yes.'

And at that moment Mrs Pel came bustling back from the direction of her small flat carrying a photograph album. 'I knew I'd find it,' she announced happily, then checked. 'Oh, Miss Ginny. Are the other guests arriving?'

'No,' Ginny assured her. 'I just remembered a few last-minute things.'

She emptied what remained of the nuts into a bowl and picked up a dish of cheese straws, intending to head for the door but something made her linger and listen.

'There she is,' Mrs Pel was saying. 'Out in the garden with Mrs Charlton. And that's her helping at the village fete. Oh, but she was a lovely girl.'

Andre Duchard said softly, '*Si jeune. Si innocente.*'

'That's what she was,' Mrs Pelham said almost fiercely. 'Not a bad bone in her body, and I'll say so until my dying day.'

And with that came the sound of the doorbell and

she became the correct housekeeper again. 'Now, if you'll excuse me, sir.'

Ginny raced ahead to the drawing room, Andre Duchard beside her, and was standing, smiling, as the Welburns were shown in.

She took a deep breath as she performed the necessary introductions, and offered drinks. Sir Malcolm and Lady Welburn both asked for sherry, while Jonathan and Andre Duchard requested Scotch.

Jonathan came with her to help with the drinks. He said in an undertone, 'This must be a nightmare.'

'Life has been easier,' she agreed quietly, at which moment the door opened and Rosina came in wearing a black silk sheath which showed off her still admirable legs, uttering smiling greetings with profuse apologies for her tardiness.

'I do hope Virginia has been looking after you properly,' she added. 'A gin and tonic for me, darling, please. And do I see it's snowing again? How very tiresome.'

Just as a slightly stilted general discussion of the weather was running out of steam, Cilla chose to arrive, halting in the doorway for maximum effect. In her violet tunic dress and black tights she looked like a particularly sexy herald, and it was clear she knew it.

Ginny found herself glancing at Andre Duchard, observing with faint alarm that his mouth was curling into amusement, and something else besides.

Not just a bad idea, this party, she thought uneasily. The worst ever.

When dinner was announced, Ginny discovered that her carefully devised seating plan had been discarded.

'No need for formality on a family occasion,' Rosina announced brightly from the head of the table, indicating that the Welburns should sit on either side of her.

Ginny saw with foreboding that Andre Duchard had adroitly taken a seat next to Cilla, leaving Jonathan to sit opposite to them.

The salmon mousse was eaten with great appreciation, Rosina blandly accepting the praise lavished on it.

'Cooking has always been one of my great pleasures,' she added.

Lady Welburn looked over her glasses. 'I thought this was one of your wonderful Mrs Pel's specialities.'

Rosina didn't miss a beat. 'I'm afraid this sort of thing is rather beyond her now. She really should have retired long since.' She turned to Ginny. 'The next course, dear. Would you mind?'

Inside the pastry case, the fillet of beef with its layer of pâté and mushrooms was cooked to pink perfection and the garlicky roasted vegetables made a delicious and colourful accompaniment.

Sir Malcolm had jovially offered to act as wine waiter, his brows lifting a little when he saw that Ginny had chosen a St Emilion to succeed the Chablis served with the first course.

'Bordeaux, my dear chap, not Burgundy,' he boomed as he filled Andre Duchard's glass. 'I hope you won't see it as a challenge.'

'By no means,' Andre returned softly, his gaze meeting Ginny's across the table. 'A wonderful wine is always that, no matter where the grape is grown.'

She flushed. 'I don't really know much about wine,' she said untruthfully, and saw his smile widen.

Lady Welburn came to her rescue. 'Where in Burgundy do you live, Monsieur Duchard?'

'A village called Terauze, *madame*.'

'Terauze?' Sir Malcolm mused. 'That name's familiar. Are you involved with the wine industry, Mr Duchard?'

'I work in the Domaine Baron Emile, *monsieur*.'

To Ginny's horror, the look Rosina sent Lady Welburn could not have stated, *A peasant. I knew it*, more obviously if she'd shouted it aloud. But her air as she turned to Andre Duchard was gracious.

'Are you one of the people who tread the grapes, Mr Duchard?'

'*Non, hélas.*' His dark face was impassive. 'They are no longer crushed in that way. Although still picked by hand.'

'Ah,' Rosina said vaguely. 'Then I suppose you have little to do at this time of year.'

'Perhaps, at this precise moment, *madame*.' He shrugged. 'But after the feast of St Vincent, the patron of *vignerons,* in ten days' time, we begin pruning.'

'Fascinating,' said Rosina, and turned back to Lady Welburn with a query about the Women's Institute.

While Andre Duchard, still smiling, resumed devoting his attention to Cilla.

Or as it was better known, blatantly flirting with her under the nose of her fiancé, thought Ginny furiously. And her 'beautiful sister' was responding, all sideways glances under her darkened lashes, and little soft giggles.

She'd once heard flirting defined as 'making love without touching' and here was a practical demonstration, as Andre Duchard smiled into Cilla's eyes. Murmured to her, his lips just a breath from her ear...

Very different, she thought, a sudden strange pain twisting inside her, to the way he treated me. Grabbing me and kissing me—like that.

Which is something I've decided not to think about again, and to behave as if it never happened.

The Welburns, she could see, were studiously pretending not to notice what was going on at the other end of the table. However, one glance at Jonathan told her he was wearing his normally pleasant expression like a mask.

She turned to him, nailing on a smile, asking him about the horse she'd heard he was buying.

'I'm paying a hefty price for it,' he returned tersely. 'I just hope it turns out to be worth it.'

Ginny found herself suddenly remembering Andre Duchard's mocking reference to village gossip about Jonathan paying for his pleasures—which she'd almost forgotten in its disturbing aftermath. Taking a deep breath, she resolved to issue a sisterly warning at the earliest convenient moment.

Every scrap of food disappeared, so Ginny presumed she was the only one who'd felt that the tender flavoursome beef was like chewing old leather gloves. And the champagne jellies decorated with frosted grapes provided a delicate and perfect finale to the meal, with only Sir Malcolm and Andre Duchard opting for cheese as well.

'Coffee in the drawing room, I think.' Rosina rose, smoothing down her dress. 'See to it, please, Virginia dear.'

Ginny suspected she was being got out of the way, but there was nothing she could do about it.

While Mrs Pel made the coffee and set the tray, she cleared the dining room table and loaded the dishwasher before setting off grimly for the drawing room, only to have her worst fears confirmed when she got to the door, and heard Rosina saying in tones of outrage, 'No? You're refusing my perfectly reasonable request without even considering it? When it was your father's express wish that Lucilla should be married from this house? That he intended to give her away?' Her voice throbbed. 'Oh, this is disgraceful—unbelievable.'

Heart sinking, Ginny pushed the door wide and

went in. Not that anyone noticed her arrival. Everyone was staring transfixed at the furious woman and cold-eyed young man confronting each other from opposite sides of the wide fireplace.

'My father's wish, *madame*?' Andre Duchard queried coldly. 'I hardly think so. Perhaps you are not aware that only a few weeks ago he arranged for this house to be leased for three years from the end of next month, or that he himself was planning to move to France. *En effet* to join me in Terauze.

'The agreement with the tenants has been signed and it would not be in my power to terminate it, even if I wished to do so.' He added flatly, 'Which I do not.'

In the astonished silence which followed, Ginny set the coffee tray down carefully before she dropped it. Keeping her hand steady, she picked up the heavy *cafetière* and began to fill the cups, her mind whirling.

Somehow, she heard herself say quietly, 'Would you like cream, Lady Welburn?'

As if a thread had been snapped, the atmosphere in the room changed from high drama to the prosaic.

Lady Welburn said gratefully, 'Thank you, my dear,' then turned to her future daughter-in-law, who had started to cry. 'Calm down, child. It's hardly the end of the world.'

'But we've ordered this really pretty marquee in pink and white stripes, and we were going to have flowers to match,' Cilla wailed. 'Oh, it's too cruel of Andrew. How could he have done such a thing, and not told us?'

Probably to avoid a scene like this, Ginny thought drily.

'Well, I don't believe a word of it,' Rosina said furiously.

Andre shrugged. 'Then I suggest you consult Monsieur Hargreaves, who will confirm the details.'

'Hargreaves?' Rosina gave a metallic laugh. 'I'll find a proper lawyer of my own who won't let me be cheated out of my rights.'

'Cheated?' Andre Duchard echoed musingly. 'Perhaps, *madame*, that is the last argument you of all people should pursue.'

Ginny saw the high colour suddenly fade from her mother's face and Sir Malcolm move quickly to her side.

'Sit down, Mrs Charlton.' He led her firmly to a chair. 'Naturally, this has all been most distressing for you, but I'm sure Andrew had every intention of discussing his plans with you, but sadly had no time to do so.

'It could have been a most exciting change for you both,' he added encouragingly. 'A whole new life.'

'Live in France? With his bastard?' Rosina's voice shook. 'I would never—never have agreed. As he should—he must have known.'

'And my wedding,' Cilla broke in with sudden energy. 'What's going to happen about my wedding—all my plans? They're ruined,' she added with a sob.

'No, Lucilla, they'll just have to be changed,' said Lady Welburn. 'Something we can discuss at another time when you are more composed.'

But Cilla was not to be pacified, glaring up at Ginny who was approaching with her coffee.

'Did you know about this? I bet you did. And you can take that away. I don't want it.' She flung out a petulant hand, knocking the cup from Ginny's grasp to the carpet, and spilling its contents down the taupe dress in the process.

Lady Welburn's mouth tightened into a line of disapproval.

She said to her husband, 'I think perhaps we should be going, my dear.'

Andre Duchard walked forward. *'Au contraire, madame.* Please do not disturb yourself. I am clearly *de trop* and the one who should leave. My apologies for spoiling a pleasant evening, although the cause of the disagreement was not of my choosing. *Bonsoir.'*

He offered a tight-lipped smile and walked to the door, where he turned to look back at Ginny, down on one knee retrieving the cup and saucer from the rug.

'I wish I could regret also the damage to your dress, *mademoiselle*,' he said softly. 'But, *hélas*, that is impossible. I see it rather as an act of God.'

And, with that, he went.

She should have felt insulted, she realised as she stared after him. Instead, incredibly, she had to fight to control the great gust of laughter suddenly welling up inside her.

'You see, Lady Welburn.' Rosina's voice throbbed into the startled silence, reminding her there was nothing to laugh about. 'You see how impossible it is to deal with this—creature. God knows what pressure he brought to bear on my poor Andrew. I know he would never have given up this house of his own free will, not when he knew how much it meant to me.'

She rounded on Ginny, who had risen to her feet, holding the unbroken china. 'This is all your fault. I knew that inviting this Duchard here would be a disaster.'

Lady Welburn rose too. She said quietly, 'I hardly think Virginia can be blamed for her late stepfather's decisions, Mrs Charlton. Like you, she probably wasn't consulted.' She paused. 'I feel we should leave you to think quietly about the situation.' She gave Ginny a kind smile. 'Why not go upstairs and take off that dress, my dear. Perhaps soak it in cold water.'

Or throw it in the bin, thought Ginny. Quite apart from its lack of appeal, it would always be a reminder of an evening best forgotten.

Up in her room, she quickly exchanged it for the ruby velvet robe which had been Andrew's last birthday gift. She'd have given anything simply to go to bed, but there was still clearing up to be done, so she waited at the top of the stairs for the Welburns to depart before she ventured down again.

But as she reached the hall, the front door opened and Jonathan came in, white flakes of snow clinging to his hair and dark overcoat.

He checked when he saw her. 'Oh, I'm sorry. Dad forgot his scarf.'

'It's there on the hall table.' She paused as he retrieved it. 'Jon, please apologise to your parents. I—I had no idea the evening would turn out like this.'

He gave a short, harsh laugh. 'That goes for me too. What on earth was Cilla doing—coming on to that man like that?'

Ginny bit her lip. 'She wanted a favour from him. Maybe she was just trying to improve relations—make him more amenable.' She tried to smile. 'You know how she is, when her heart's set on something.'

'I'm beginning to,' he said. 'But after tonight, I'm not entirely convinced that it's me.'

Ginny groaned under her breath. This was serious stuff.

She said, 'Jon, you can't really believe that. Cilla interested in someone like Andre Duchard? Never in a million years. She may have behaved unwisely at dinner, but none of us are altogether rational at the moment.'

She added vehemently, 'Besides, no one in her right mind could ever prefer him to you.'

He said more gently, 'You're a good friend, Ginny. Better than I deserve, I think.'

He bent suddenly and to her surprise and alarm she felt his lips touch hers. It was only a fleeting caress, but she stepped back instantly, aware as she did so of a sound like the soft closing of a nearby door.

She forced a smile. 'And I'll be an even greater sister-in-law. Goodnight, Jon, and don't worry. Everything will work out just fine. You'll see.'

She saw him out, and locked up, remembering as she did so the time before Cilla had returned and taken him captive. When she'd hoped that one day he might take her in his arms and kiss her.

And now, suddenly, it had happened. Jon had kissed her—and she'd felt—what? Just a vague embarrassment, if she was honest, plus a deep relief that neither Cilla nor her mother had chosen to walk into the hall at that inopportune moment.

I think quite enough hell has broken loose for one day, she thought.

While tomorrow I have to go to work—and tell Miss Finn the bad news. And, for me, that's the worst prospect of all.

CHAPTER FOUR

GINNY WOKE THE following morning to find the world covered in a blanket of snow. Not enough to cause major disruption, but sufficient to be annoying, she thought as, wrapped up and booted, she took Barney for an early walk on the common.

He clearly thought the snow was wonderful and bounded round happily. On their return, he shot into the kitchen and through the door into the hall where he was shaking himself vigorously at the exact moment that Rosina was descending the stairs.

'That dog,' she exclaimed with real venom as Ginny arrived in pursuit. 'He's going just as soon as the vet can come for him.'

'No, you can't do that.' Ginny caught Barney's collar and quietened him. 'Andrew loved him.'

'More than he loved any of us, apparently,' her mother snapped.

'At least let me try and get him another home,' Ginny pleaded.

'You have a week,' Rosina flung over her shoulder as she headed for the dining room. 'Until then, he can stay in one of the outhouses. I don't want to set eyes on him again.'

And I didn't want to wake up this morning, Ginny thought wearily, towing the reluctant Barney back to the kitchen. I now see how right I was.

She'd had a restless and miserable night. As she'd guessed, Rosina and Cilla, when she'd re-joined them, had been full of their grievances, admittedly with some justice after this new thunderbolt.

Andrew must have been making his plans for a long time, she thought unhappily, and there was no doubt he'd deceived them all. Yet, at the same time, she could not forget Andre Duchard's harsh and unexpected riposte to her mother when she'd mentioned cheating.

I should have asked her about it, she told herself, and I will when I get the opportunity.

But at least Rosina seemed to accept the inevitability of Keeper's Cottage and had even agreed, grudgingly, to look it over, armed with Ginny's list of suggested refurbishments.

Now Barney, who seemed briefly to have regained some of his former exuberance, had become another addition to her list of problems, she realised unhappily as she changed into a chestnut tweed skirt and a black polo-necked sweater for work.

She had her interview with Emma Finn during her lunch break, and it was just as difficult as she'd feared.

'There's been a lot of gossip about Mr Charlton's will, as I'm sure you know,' her boss told her unhappily. 'But, frankly, I discounted it.'

'Unfortunately, it's all true.' Ginny looked down at her tightly clasped hands. 'I—I have no claim at all.'

'You don't think the new heir would back you? If you explained the circumstances?'

Ginny sat up very straight. 'I'm sure he wouldn't,' she returned with emphasis. 'Even if I could bring myself to ask him.'

'Oh, dear,' said Emma. 'Well, Ginny, I won't pretend I'm not disappointed, but Iris's offer is on the table and I need to close the deal quickly.' She frowned. 'Even though I suspect when I'm gone, it will be all change.'

Like so much else, thought Ginny as she went back to work.

It was a busy afternoon, the miserable weather creating a high demand for soup and hot chocolate as the comfort foods of choice, and everyone she served told her how sorry they were about Andrew and what a loss it was, and she quietly agreed, thanking them for their sympathy, while trying not to resent the curiosity which accompanied it.

It was only natural, she reminded herself. Andrew seemed the last man in the world to have fathered an illegitimate son, and kept him a secret all these years.

As closing time approached, Ginny was on her own in the café, clearing tables, when Andre Duchard walked in and took a seat in the corner.

For a moment, she stood, frozen, aware of the dull heavy thunder of her heart, and the sudden dryness of her mouth. Real but inexplicable.

And there was nothing she could do, pride forbidding her to pick up her loaded tray and scuttle with it into the kitchen, leaving someone else to deal with the unwelcome customer.

She drew a deep breath, then walked across the room, acutely aware that he was watching her approach every step of the way, his hard mouth smiling faintly as he leaned back in his Windsor chair.

As she reached the table, he said softly, 'So this is how you pass your days.'

'Yes, it is.' Ginny lifted her chin, thankful for

the steadiness of her voice. Even investing it with a note of tartness. 'Is that what you came here for—to satisfy your curiosity?'

'*Pas entièrement.*' He gave the menu a cursory glance. '*Un café filtre, s'il vous plaît.*'

'Certainly.' She wrote on her order pad, then paused. 'Milk and sugar?'

He grimaced slightly. '*Merci.* But, perhaps, a cognac.'

Ginny shook her head. 'We aren't licensed to sell alcohol.' She added coolly, 'Not even wine, if you were hoping Miss Finn might be a potential buyer.'

'*Quel dommage,*' he said lightly and looked down at the menu again. 'But then, this is a very feminine establishment, *n'est ce pas*?'

'Not exclusively,' she denied swiftly. 'Our food appeals to men as well.'

Although it reluctantly occurred to her that none of their other male customers brought this kind of presence—this raw energy into the place, making it seem somehow—diminished.

She found the realisation disturbing, and hurried into speech again. 'Maybe you should stick to the Rose and Crown.'

He shrugged. 'Its coffee does not deserve the

name. But it serves its purpose in other ways. I have found it *une veritable mine de renseignements.*'

He paused, observing her puzzled expression. 'A mine of information,' he explained. He gave her an ironic look. 'Also the girls who work there smile more.'

Ginny stiffened. 'Perhaps they have more to be happy about. You seem to forget that I have lost someone I looked on as a father for a lot of years.'

'As I did not,' he said with a touch of harshness. 'For most of my life, he was just a name. And when that changed, at first I did not welcome it.'

'Whereas we weren't even aware you existed.'

He said drily, 'And you wish it had stayed that way, *n'est-ce pas*?'

'I certainly wish we'd been prepared,' she returned stonily. 'Instead of being subjected to one shock after another.'

'And you hate him for this?'

She gave him a startled look. 'No—no, of course not. How could I?' She paused. 'I just don't understand how he could have kept all this from us for so long.'

He said softly, 'But we all have our secrets, do we not? Matters we prefer to keep from the world?' For a second his reflective gaze lingered on her parted lips, as if reminding her of those brief devastating moments in his arms, and to her fury, Ginny felt her skin warm in a response she was unable to control.

'As for my father...' He shrugged again. 'Perhaps, he believed there would always be more time—to explain the past and talk of his plans for the future. A lesson we should value, *peut-être.*'

'Just as I should remember I'm here to work,' she said curtly, still feeling off-balance and hating him for it. 'I'll get your coffee, Monsieur Duchard.'

'And bring one for yourself. I wish to speak with you.'

'That's against the rules. We don't sit with the customers.'

His brows lifted mockingly. '*Oh là là.* Not even when it is with a member of the family?'

'You and I are in no way related,' she said. Adding, 'Thankfully.'

'Then we agree on something, *enfin.*' He smiled at her. 'Now, for once, break this rule that I do not believe exists, and drink coffee with me.' He added drily, 'On the understanding, *bien sûr,* that we do not throw it over each other.'

Ginny sent him a fulminating glance then went reluctantly to the hotplate behind the counter and poured two black coffees, aware she was under scrutiny through the glazed panel at the top of the kitchen door.

There was a large mirror on the back wall, and she caught a glimpse of herself as she turned, all shiny face and hair in lank wisps.

She looked like someone who'd been on her feet all day—and in a menial job at that, while the butcher's apron made her feel suddenly like a badly wrapped parcel.

But what the hell, she thought. He has no illusions about me. He came here to talk, that's all.

Her hands were shaking, in an echo of the foolish inner turmoil she seemed unable to control, but she managed to get the cups back to the table without spilling any of the liquid in the saucers.

'What did you want to discuss?' she asked, perching awkwardly on the edge of her chair.

'Let us begin with your extraordinary wish to buy this business.'

She put her cup down quickly. 'How did you know about that?'

'My father told me.' He paused. 'Please understand that he did not wish to disappoint you, but he did not favour the proposal.'

'He told you that?' Mortified, Ginny swallowed. 'But—why?'

'He did not want you to be the next Miss Finn. He thought you too young to bury yourself in such a future.'

She bit her lip. 'Well, it hardly matters. The café's being sold to someone else.'

'So you will be looking for a fresh start, away from here, *peut-être.*'

She said shortly, 'I haven't decided.'

His mouth curled slightly. 'No doubt there is much to consider. But I advise you to ignore your mother's hopes of having my father's will set aside in her favour. It will not happen, no matter what *avocat* she chooses to employ in place of Monsieur Hargreaves.'

'In his place?' Ginny was bewildered. 'I don't understand.'

'They spoke on the telephone today. She was angry he had not warned her that the house had been rented. He explained that he had not wished to immediately burden her with more bad news. That he awaited only a convenient opportunity. But it made no difference. She no longer wishes him to act for her.'

Stifling a groan, she said, 'I'm sure she didn't mean it. I'll talk to her.'

'I think it is too late for that. She blames him, *tu comprends*, for obeying my father's instructions about the disposal of his estate. For not, as she says, making him see reason.'

The note of faint derision in his voice flicked Ginny on the raw. She said hotly, 'Clearly you don't understand how my mother feels. How bewildered—how hurt she is—to be treated like this—after eleven happy years.'

'That is how you see it? *Une vraie idylle?*' The mockery was overt now and it stung. 'Which is how it began, *n'est-ce pas*? The deck of a ship beneath the stars—a man and a woman in each other's arms, overcoming past tragedy, finding new hope together?'

'And what's wrong with that?' Ginny demanded defensively. 'Lots of people begin lasting relationships on holiday.'

He said softly, 'And many more treat it as an enjoyable interlude, and never think of it again on their return to the lives they live each day. Perhaps that is the wisest course.'

She stared at him. 'And that's what you think my mother should have done?'

His tone hardened. 'I cannot speak for her. But my father—*certainement.*'

She said, 'I think you're being insulting.'

He shrugged. 'I would say—truthful.'

Ginny got to her feet, trembling. 'What right have you to judge her—or any of us? My mother was left a widow with two young children, and very little money.'

His mouth twisted cynically. 'Yet she was a partner in a beauty salon, *n'est-ce pas,* and could afford to pay for an expensive cruise in the Mediterranean, on which she did not choose to include you or your sister. *Incroyable.*'

Partner in a beauty salon? Ginny repeated silently, her heart missing a beat. Her mother had been a manicurist. An employee. What was he talking about?

She hastily switched tack. 'You speak as if my mother abandoned us in the streets,' she challenged. 'We actually stayed with my godmother and her husband in Fulham, and had a wonderful time, whereas we'd have been bored stiff on a ship all day long.

'And Mother was only able to go on the cruise because she won a prize in the National Lottery. Not one of the big ones, of course,' she added quickly, seeing his brows lift. 'But it paid for all sorts of things. Besides, she'd had a tough time and she needed a break.'

'*Sans doute.*' His voice was flat. 'And, at the end of the cruise, *quelle surprise,* she has a new and wealthy husband.'

Her voice shook. 'How dare you. What the hell are you implying?'

'I imply nothing. I state facts. Can you deny that you have ever wondered how it came about—this so convenient marriage?'

'Of course I deny it. They met and fell in love. That's all there is to it.' She gripped the back of her chair with both hands as pain, a strange mixture of hurt and bewilderment, twisted inside her, adding to her shock and confusion. 'Is this the kind of poison you've been feeding to Andrew over the years? Turning him against his own wife? Well, I won't—I don't believe a word of it.'

'A display of family loyalty?' he countered harshly. 'A little late for that, I think. And I said nothing to my father. *Au contraire,* the doubts were all his own. You are not a fool, Virginie, so ask yourself why.'

He drained his cup and rose, dropping a hand-

ful of pound coins on the table. 'But your coffee
is excellent,' he added, and walked out.

She wanted to fling the money after him, but
her awareness of the watchers in the kitchen pre-
vented her.

She put the payment for the coffee in the till and
dropped the rest into the jar for staff tips, then carried her laden tray into the kitchen, ignoring the
curious glances which greeted her.

And she hadn't been able to talk to him about
Barney and her plan to rehome him, she realised
ruefully. But what the hell? She'd go ahead anyway.

When she got home, she found Rosina bristling
with defiance and clearly in no mood to answer
the kind of questions that Ginny knew needed to
be asked.

'I'll find a law firm in London who'll act for me,'
she declared. 'That Hargreaves man couldn't fight
his way out of a paper bag as I told him.'

Ginny bit her lip. 'Court battles are very expensive.' *Not to mention the kinds of unexpected truths
that sometimes emerge as a result...*

'But my costs will be paid by the other side,'
Rosina insisted. 'And while it's all *sub judice,* I

shall insist on remaining here. I've no intention of moving into that ghastly little house.'

'It needs work,' Ginny admitted reluctantly. 'But it could be really cosy.'

Ouch, she thought, as her mother reared up indignantly. Wrong word.

'Cosy? There isn't space to swing a cat, let alone entertain my friends.' She added sharply, 'And, of course, with only two bedrooms, you'll need to find somewhere else to live.'

Ginny stared at her. 'But Cilla's getting married. Surely we can share a room until then.'

'Don't be silly, Virginia. Both bedrooms are tiny, and your sister will need storage for her clothes.' Rosina made it sound so logical. 'Anyway, it's time you were independent. You can't expect me to support you for the rest of your life.'

Ginny wanted to protest. To say, If I'd gone to university and trained as a teacher I'd be qualified by now. But you stopped me.

Instead, she said quietly, 'No, Mother. I've never expected that. And I'll find something.' She paused. 'Where is Cilla, by the way?'

'Out.' Rosina shrugged. 'I suppose at the Welburns'.'

'Building bridges, I hope,' said Ginny, remembering without pleasure that awkward few minutes with Jonathan in the hall.

'That's hardly necessary. Not when you're as pretty as Cilla.' Her mother shook her head. 'Poor Virginia. You've never really understood how it all works, have you?'

'Obviously not, but I'm learning fast.' Ginny got up. 'I think I'll have a hot bath.'

In the hall, she encountered the housekeeper. 'I won't want dinner, Mrs Pel. I'm planning an early night.'

Closing my eyes. Blotting out this awful day...

'I'm not surprised,' Mrs Pel said with faint asperity. 'You look washed out. But you're not going to bed hungry,' she added firmly. 'I'll bring you something on a tray.'

The 'something' turned out to be a steaming bowl of Scotch broth, accompanied by crusty bread, a hunk of cheese and an apple, and this, allied with the hot-water bottle Ginny had discovered in her bed, made her throat tighten with the threat of tears.

But I can't cry, she thought. Because if I start, I may never stop, and I need to be strong.

'You're spoiling me, Mrs Pel,' she said with an attempt at lightness.

'It doesn't happen so often.' The older woman set the tray across Ginny's lap. 'Besides, it may be my last chance to do so. Mrs Charlton wants me gone by the end of the week.'

'The end of the week,' Ginny repeated numbly. 'But that isn't even proper notice.'

'Oh, hush now,' Mrs Pel said robustly. 'She's been trying to get rid of me for long enough, as well you know. And I've no wish to stay on here without the master, not with my beautiful cottage waiting for me.'

She paused. 'And you should do the same, my dear. Spread your wings and fly.'

She gave a brisk nod and left Ginny to her supper. And to her thoughts—which, although confused and unhappy, were still not proof against the delicious soup, thick with chunks of lamb, vegetables and pearl barley, and spreading its beguiling warmth through every inch of her. She found she was finishing every last drop and scraping the bowl.

She finished off the bread with the cheese, then, leaning back against her pillows, began to eat the apple, juicy and slightly tart, just as she'd always liked them. Like the ones on the tree in Aunt Joy's garden at the big comfortable house in Fulham…

She hadn't thought about that for years, and but for Andre Duchard's hateful insinuations, she wouldn't be remembering any of it now. Yet some of their exchange had set alarm bells ringing. And taken her unwillingly back to the time when she was eleven years old and her life had changed for ever.

Taking her back to Lorimer Street. A terraced house like all its neighbours with a small paved area in front and a yard at the back.

A house her mother had always hated, although Ginny could recall her father explaining quietly and patiently that on his present salary as a primary school teacher, it was all they could afford. That when he got promotion, they could, perhaps, think again.

Instead he'd become ill, and while Ginny had been too young to understand what leukaemia was, some instinct had told her that it was taking her gentle, humorous father away from her, all too quickly and with a terrible finality.

A trained beautician, Rosina had been working part-time at a local salon but switched to full-time when she became a widow. The wages, bolstered by tips from a wealthy clientele, weren't generous, but the family survived, with the help of neighbours in term time and Aunt Joy in the school holidays.

She could remember taking Cilla to the salon each day after school, keeping her quiet in the cramped staffroom with crayons and colouring books until it was time to go home.

'She's your little sister,' her mother had told her. 'It's your job to look after her.' And she'd obeyed.

Aunt Joy and her husband, who owned a successful garage chain, were childless, but they were always genuinely delighted to see Rosina and her daughters, although Ginny had noticed that her mother was often quiet—almost brooding—on their return to Lorimer Street, as if she was making comparisons between their differing lifestyles, and finding them odious.

Just as she did when the clients at the salon talked about their villas on the Mediterranean and showed off their new jewellery and designer dresses.

Then one day Rosina was suddenly the one with carrier bags full of clothes from Oxford Street and Knightsbridge.

'I've had a surprise,' she told them airily. 'A little windfall.'

Not so little, thought Ginny. Several thousand pounds from the Lottery. Enough to pay for a cruise in the sun and more while she and Cilla stayed with Aunt Joy.

They'd known exactly when their mother was returning by the days crossed off from the kitchen calendar. Ginny watched them mount up, longing to go back to Lorimer Street and their usual life.

But when Rosina returned, it was not to Lorimer Street. Instead she'd taken a short-term rental on an attractive flat in a modern block. And after Aunt Joy had delivered them there, they'd heard the sounds of her quarrelling with their mother and then the distant slamming of a door.

Even then she hadn't moved, just waited until her mother came, flushed and tight-mouthed, her voice brittle as she said, 'Let's explore our new palace.'

Holding Cilla's hand, she trailed obediently in Rosina's wake through the spacious sitting room, the beautiful ivory and aqua master bedroom, the sumptuous bathroom with its pink and violet tiles, and the chrome and marble kitchen, and all she could think was how much she hated it.

'When are we going back to Lorimer Street?' she'd asked at last.

'We're not,' her mother said shortly. 'There is no Lorimer Street. I don't want to hear you talk about it again. Ever.'

And she meant it, thought Ginny, feeling the same little shiver drift down her spine. She made it seem as if that other life had never existed. Just as we never heard from Aunt Joy and Uncle Harry again. And I was not allowed to mention them either.

Then, one afternoon, Rosina had taken them out to tea in a big department store.

Ginny could remember how Rosina had gripped their hands as if she was nervous as they emerged from the lift, until a tall grey-haired man, at a table on his own, stood up smiling, when she'd relaxed and smiled back.

'Darlings,' she said. 'This is a very special friend of mine.'

And that, thought Ginny, was our first meeting with Andrew.

Frowning, she transferred her supper tray to the bedside table and sat up, hugging her knees.

It was clear that Rosina had improved on her employment status and rented the flat to impress the new man in her life.

Not strictly ethical perhaps, she thought defensively, but hardly federal offences. Or enough to make her husband feel cheated, if he'd ever found out.

Besides, to set against all that, Rosina, in her thirties, had been and even now continued to be a beautiful woman, her hair still fair—admittedly with assistance these days—and her skin flawless.

Small wonder that Andrew had been sufficiently attracted to offer marriage.

And even if their life together hadn't been perfect, it was surely better than a lot of marriages.

So Andre Duchard had no right to imply anything different. No right at all.

The best thing I can do, she told herself resolutely, is put the whole business—especially him—out of my mind. And concentrate instead on whatever the future holds for me.

And tried not to think how bleak that sounded.

CHAPTER FIVE

OVER THE NEXT couple of days, Ginny's misgivings over her prospects at Miss Finn's began to multiply, with Iris Potter talking openly about the changes she was planning.

But at least Andre Duchard had not returned, to Ginny's relief, although she was aware that every time the bell tinkled on the café door to signal a new arrival, her heart seemed to do a kind of somersault, which made no sense at all.

For all she knew, he might be back in Burgundy and good riddance to him. The last person she needed to have around was someone who caught her so consistently off her guard. Who'd forced her to remember things much better forgotten. And, even worse, who'd made her aware of feelings she'd infinitely have preferred to have ignored. He was altogether too disturbing.

But much as she wished him gone, some instinct told her that he was still around. And still able to push her towards some unsuspected edge…

Stop it, she adjured herself, digging her nails into the palms of her hands. Don't think like that. In fact, don't think about him at all.

Rosina was still hunting obsessively on the telephone for the legal advice she wanted to hear, and not even the start of the improvements to Keeper's Cottage was able to divert her.

On the contrary, Ginny told herself grimly, Rosina still seemed hell-bent on staying exactly where she was.

And her attitude to Barney had not softened either.

'Have you done anything about finding him a new owner, Virginia? If not, at the end of the week—he goes.'

'I've put a card in the newsagent's window,' Ginny said quietly.

'You think you'll be inundated with replies?' Rosina gave a short laugh. 'I doubt it.'

'I'd settle for one person who really wants him,' Ginny returned. And, if it was humanly possible, that would be me, she thought now with a pang, deciding she would pop up to the shop during her meal break to check.

But it was after two o'clock before Ginny was

able to hang up her apron, fling on her coat and sprint up the High Street to Betts Newsagents.

Only to meet with another disappointment.

'It's a bad time of year to be taking on a dog, what with Christmas bills coming in, and nasty weather for walking,' said Mrs Betts. 'I'd hang on for spring, Miss Mason, and try again.'

If only, thought Ginny as she turned away, with a word of thanks and a forced smile.

As she emerged from the shop and caught sight of the timbered façade of the Rose and Crown directly opposite, rising anger fought her initial sense of defeat.

There he was, she thought, fiercely. The man who'd appeared from nowhere, been given everything yet seemed to value none of it.

She was turning to go back to the café when her eye was caught by a splash of colour and she saw a figure in a familiar quilted jacket the colour of violets emerge almost furtively through the archway which led to the hotel entrance, pulling her fur-trimmed hood forward as if to shield her face as well as cover her blonde hair.

Ginny stood, her breathing as laboured as if she'd been punched in the chest, watching Cilla, head bent, pick her way carefully down the slushy pavement towards the turning for the car park, and disappear from view.

No. The word echoed in Ginny's head with such force that for a terrible moment she thought she'd shouted it out loud. But no passers-by turned to stare, so she stayed where she was under the shelter of Mrs Betts' awning, trying to pull herself together.

Telling herself there had to be a dozen innocent reasons for Cilla to visit the Rose and Crown, but unable to think of one. It was just the village local, and her sister's preference was for upmarket country pubs with interesting menus and an expensive wine list.

The kind of places Jonathan took her to...

She swallowed, remembering the dinner party. Andre Duchard leaning towards her sister, dark gaze intent, murmuring heaven knows what. And Cilla smiling, lapping up the attention. Maybe thinking she had him eating out of the palm of her hand. And all the time, oblivious to Jonathan's irritation and resentment.

But surely—*surely*—it had stopped there. It must have done, she argued to herself. Because Cilla couldn't possibly have arranged to meet Andre secretly—could she?

Did she have some hare-brained idea that she could persuade him somehow to arrange for her to use Barrowdean House for the wedding after all?

Persuade him somehow...

Ginny felt sick under the force of the emotions churning inside her—the predominant one, she told herself, being anger.

Didn't Cilla see that if Jonathan, already jealous, even suspected she'd been slipping off to meet Andre Duchard on the quiet, there would be no wedding? She must be crazy to take such a risk.

So, whatever was going on had to stop right there before Cilla made an irretrievable ruin of her life.

She's still my little sister, she thought, swallowing. And I have to look after her.

Almost before she realised what she was doing, she'd crossed the road and walked into hotel reception. There was no one at the desk but one glance at the board where the keys hung told her that only Room 3 was missing.

Unseen and unheard, she went up the stairs two at a time. The room she wanted was at the end of the corridor, and a 'Do Not Disturb' sign hung from the door handle.

No prizes for guessing why, Ginny thought savagely, clenching her fist and rapping loudly on the wooden panels. Oh, Cilla, you *fool*...

And with that, the door was flung open and Andre Duchard confronted her. Apart from a towel knotted round his waist and a scowl, he was wearing nothing. And the scowl intensified as he looked down at her.

'You,' he ground out. 'What are you doing here? What do you want?' His hair was wet and tangled and his shoulders, torso and long muscular legs also gleamed with the sheen of water. Stubble darkened his chin.

Aware that there was altogether too much of him on show, Ginny, pulses hammering, elected for safety and looked him in the eye. She said with stinging emphasis, 'I want you to leave my sister alone. Non-negotiable.'

'Your sister?' he repeated. 'What are you saying?'

'Oh, don't pretend.' Looking past him, Ginny could see the tumbled bed in the light of the shaded lamp on the night table. Her throat tightened uncontrollably, making her voice husky. 'She was here this afternoon. At the hotel. I saw her leaving.'

'And from that you deduce—*quoi*?' He seized her wrist with one hand, drawing her forward into the room, and slammed the door with the other. Shutting them in together.

She wrenched free. 'What the hell are you doing?' Her voice quivered.

'I think it is called conversation,' he said. 'In private.' The dark gaze pinned her like a butterfly to a cork. 'So you think she has been with me, and we are lovers?'

Ginny swallowed, trying to control the flurry of her breathing. The room, not large at the best of times, seemed to be humming with anger, which closed round her oppressively, making her want to step back, away from him.

Away, too, from the frankly enticing scent of soap and shampoo emanating from his cool, damp skin. But that would take her nearer to the bed, so she stood her ground. Because she was the one with the right to be angry. And she needed to stay angry.

She said defiantly, 'You find her attractive. Your behaviour the other night made that perfectly clear. And she hasn't had a great deal of experience of men, so she'll have been flattered. But she's engaged—in love.' She added with energy, 'And I won't let her screw up her life just so that you can satisfy a passing fancy.'

'Engaged, *certainement.* At least for the present. In love?' He shrugged. 'Who knows? I think you are the one who is naïve, Virginie.'

He paused.

'But let us be frank. Would it not make you happy if the young Monsieur Welburn, the rich and worthy, was no longer your sister's fiancé and could, *peut-être,* return for consolation to the girl he chose first—*toi-même.*'

He added harshly, 'Now you are the one who must not pretend. Or did you think your so tender and half-dressed embrace with him that night had been unobserved?'

She remembered the sound of the closing door. She said hoarsely, 'You—were there?'

'I had been saying goodnight to Marguerite. When I saw that I intruded, I left another way.'

Ginny lifted her chin. She said with cool clarity, 'There was no intrusion. What you saw was perfectly innocent. He'd had a wretched evening, and was—upset, that's all.'

His mouth twisted cynically. 'And when they are married, he and your sister, and all his evenings become wretched, who will he turn to then? Because *la belle Lucille,* she requires a stronger man than the unfortunate Jonathan. Someone who will not indulge her foolishly, but give purpose to her life each day, and teach her to be a woman in his bed at night.'

She stiffened. 'I suppose you're referring to yourself with all this macho nonsense.'

The dark brows lifted. 'And if so, why should you care? I would be doing you a favour, *n'est ce pas*? Is that not what you want?'

Her mouth felt suddenly dry. She touched her lips with the tip of her tongue, as she searched for a reply. Any reply, as the silence in the room lengthened. Tautened. Began to spark with emotions that had nothing to do with the anger which had brought her here like an avenging Fury. And which scared her.

She thought with swift desperation, What am I doing—challenging him like this? I should have spoken to Cilla instead. I must be crazy...

In a voice she did not recognise, she said, 'I shouldn't have come here. I'm sorry. I—I have to go...'

To get out of here while I still can...

She took a step towards the door, but he remained where he was, blocking her path.

'Not,' he said, 'until you have answered my question. And told me the truth.' The dark eyes bored into hers. 'So, say it to me—what do you most want, Virginie?'

She looked away, trembling. 'I—I can't tell you.' She moved her hands almost helplessly, as she faced the shocking truth he had demanded. 'Because I—I just don't know any more.'

'Then I, *moi-même*, shall tell you.' His voice was a harsh whisper. He reached for her, pushing her coat from her shoulders, letting it tumble to the carpet, then pulled her close, his mouth seeking hers with a hunger that would not be denied.

She knew a moment of blind panic, telling herself to fight. To kick his bare legs with her heavy shoes. Rake his face and chest with her nails. Anything to get free—to be safe again.

Yet, somehow, she did none of those things. Because she would also be fighting herself, she realised in some dazed corner of her mind. Because, to her bewilderment and eternal shame, she knew that she shared his hunger, swaying against him, her lips parting under his to allow him the access he demanded.

This can't—this mustn't happen. The words might echo in her head, but their warning was soon drowned by the mounting urgency in her body, in the heavy thud of her pulses, the sensation that the blood in her veins was flowing slow and sweet, like honey.

She leaned into him, welcoming the heated tangle of his tongue with hers, shivering at the glide of his hands under her sweater and across the supple line of her back. Admitting that this was what she'd wanted since the first time he'd kissed her.

Deftly, he unhooked her bra, his fingers pushing aside the loosened lace cups to encompass the warm, firm roundness of her small breasts, his thumbs teasing her nipples until they stood proud and erect, making her gasp with shocked pleasure against his smile.

He pulled her sweater over her head and tossed it to the floor, sending her bra to follow it, then held her to him closely, tightly, kissing her ever more deeply.

For the first time in her life, she experienced the excitement—the incitement—of a man's hair-roughened chest grazing her naked breasts, and she melted into him, returning his kisses with untutored ardour.

She was dizzily aware of him releasing the zip on her dark green cord skirt, pushing the fabric over her hips, and down to the ground. He lifted her free of the encumbering pool of fabric, letting her shoes fall at the same time, leaving her in nothing but her tights and briefs. Pulling her hips forward so that her body ground against his, showing in no uncertain terms that he was starkly and formidably aroused.

A demonstration, however, that also served to remind her of her own sexual inexperience and lack of sophistication.

And as if he sensed her sudden uncertainty, his hold relaxed a little. His fingers lifted to stroke the silken fall of her brown hair, then cupped the nape of her neck, bringing her mouth slowly and warmly back to his. Kissing her again, but this time softly and languorously. Endlessly.

And as he did so, his hands moved on her very gently, exploring each delicate curve and angle, his fingertips caressing her throat, her slender shoulder blades, the soft flesh of her inner arms before returning to her breasts and lifting them to the silken warmth of his mouth.

And as his tongue flickered lightly, devastatingly on the engorged rosy peaks, Ginny felt her body clench, fiercely and exquisitely, in response. Telling her that this was no longer enough.

Reminding her too that, through her own choice, the point of no return was long past.

Self-doubt forgotten, she twined her arms round his neck, burying her face in his bare shoulder as he picked her up in his arms and carried her to the bed, tossing aside the rumpled covers, and lowering her to the mattress.

The bed dipped as he joined her, his towel now discarded, bending over her, slowly peeling away her tights and the briefs she wore beneath them, uncovering her completely to the breathtaking urgency of his hands caressing her flat abdomen, exploring the hollows of her pelvis and moving downwards to hover tantalisingly at the soft brown triangle at the joining of her thighs.

She gasped, arching towards him, as she yielded herself to this new intimacy, trembling as he began to trace a slow lingering path over the slick, wet heat of her womanhood, each sensuous movement of his fingers making her quiver with sensation, revealing within her an undreamed of capacity for arousal.

She touched him too, smoothing her fingers in wonderment across his skin, learning the unfamiliar male shape from the broad muscular shoulders down to the narrow hips and firm, flat buttocks. And he captured her hand and kissed it and brought it to his body, clasping it round his jutting hardness, letting her feel the size and strength of him stir and lift under her first tentative caresses.

At the same time his fingers were still exploring her—slowly—exquisitely. Finding her most sensitive place, and hovering there, teasing the tiny bud into swollen, aching excitement.

She gave a tiny breathless moan, looking up into his face, her eyes widening under her long lashes, as she saw his own gaze deepen in purpose and intensity. As she felt him move over her, his hands sliding under her slender flanks and lifting her to him.

His voice was a harsh whisper. 'Take me, *ma douce, ma belle.*'

And she obeyed, wordlessly, guiding him to her. Into her willing warmth...

She had not expected there to be pain, yet there was and she found herself sinking her teeth into her lower lip, in order to stifle her instinctive cry of protest. Aware just the same, that her need— her longing to know and be known—was all that truly mattered.

She gripped his shoulders, rearing up and thrusting herself against him, wrapping her slim legs round his hips, and felt her untried flesh yield in welcome as he filled her totally.

Locked with her, his mouth again joined to hers, Andre began to move, slowly at first then faster, the strong, rhythmic strokes of his body robbing her of what little self-control was left to her, and carrying her to some new level in a long dark spiral of mounting pleasure.

Oh, God, she thought, a sob rising in her throat. What was she letting him do to her—this man— half angel, half devil? As if he had always known how it would be between them? And as if she had ever had a choice?

And then coherent thought fled, and nothing was left but a fierce crescendo of wild, irresistible sensation, which, as she reached its peak, tossed her into one rippling, rapturous convulsion after another, making her cry out helplessly against his mouth.

And heard him answer her hoarsely as his own body juddered to its climax.

Afterwards, as he held her, both of them drained and spent, there was silence and a sense of great peace. She knew that there were things that must be said, but there was time for that, she thought, head cradled on his chest and her eyelids drooping wearily. All the time in the world.

And let that world quietly slip away.

* * *

She awoke slowly to darkness and for a moment lay still, completely disorientated. Her first realisation was that she ached deep inside her. Her second—that a heavy weight lay across her breasts, pinning her to the bed.

She turned her head gently, almost fearfully, and saw Andre Duchard's dark head on the pillow beside her. Discovered that it was his arm, thrown over her body in a kind of careless possession, that was imprisoning her.

And with that, every searing memory of the past few hours returned, screaming at her, jolting her back to the terrible—the shameful reality of what she had done.

And the absolute necessity of distancing herself from him. In every possible way. Permanently. And immediately…

Moving with the utmost caution, she was able to shift his arm sufficiently to enable her to slide towards the edge of the bed. He muttered something, and she froze, but he was only turning over and didn't wake.

Ginny didn't dare relight the lamp, which meant she had to search around on the floor in the dark for the clothing that she'd allowed—oh, God, that she'd *wanted* him to strip from her—and huddle into it as best and as soundlessly as she could.

She checked her purse and keys were still safely in her coat pocket then let herself warily out into the corridor. A glance at her watch revealed to her horror that she'd been with Andre Duchard for over two and a half hours, and quite apart from the ethical implications of her behaviour, she'd missed almost the entire afternoon session at Miss Finn's.

Although that was the least of her problems, she thought as she tiptoed down the stairs, hoping and praying there was no one at the hotel desk.

Luckily, the receptionist was again in the rear office, this time intent on her computer so Ginny was able to make her escape unobserved.

As her sister had done earlier...

The thought stopped her in her tracks. She paused in the archway, leaning against the stonework, fighting the nausea threatening to overwhelm her. Because what she'd done wasn't simply immoral—it was sheer insanity.

From the first, Andre Duchard had scarcely bothered to conceal that he despised them all. Now he had even more reason for his contempt. Because however badly Cilla had behaved, there'd been no need to emulate her.

She swallowed, making herself move. Start putting one foot in front of the other for the journey home.

She'd gone to his room supposedly seething in righteous fury on her sister's behalf only to emerge with even greater ignominy. Because he'd seen through the indignation and angry protests and recognised, as she had not, that under all the fire and fury, what she really wanted was to get laid.

Some sexual clock she'd never suspected must have been ticking.

And he'd obliged her.

She couldn't think of it in any other way, which was probably wise.

Two sisters in his bed in the same afternoon. Encounters that had not appeared to test his stamina at all, she thought, feeling as if shame was flaying the skin from her body.

A situation, in fact, that he might have found cynically amusing, as well as confirming his low opinion of her family, this time deservedly. Because she could condone Cilla's behaviour even less than her own.

I've only harmed myself—betrayed my self-respect, she thought, feeling sick. Something I can neither explain nor excuse, but shall just have to live with, somehow.

But Cilla's been unfaithful to Jonathan—the man she loves and plans to marry. So how can she ever forgive herself?

While Andre Duchard had the unmitigated, hypocritical gall to castigate me for that—goodnight peck, she told herself, biting at her already tender mouth.

When she got back to the house, she was thankful to find it deserted and went straight to her room.

She stripped and went into the shower, using a massage sponge soaked in gel to scrub every inch of her body, trying to remove any lingering evidence of his hands and mouth.

If only it was as easy to clear the memory of his touch from her brain, she thought as she shampooed her hair, letting the hot water cascade over her until every vestige of foam had gone. To forget how it felt to have him sheathed inside her. To erase the recollection of the pleasure, which still had the power to make her tremble.

She dried herself, rubbed scented lotion into her skin, put on her robe and then, at last, looked at herself in the mirror, wondering how to disguise the total giveaway of the haunted eyes and swollen mouth.

In a few short hours, she thought dispassionately, she had become a stranger to herself, not just physically but emotionally.

The girl whose life she'd been living for twenty-two years had never believed that the world was well lost for lust. Nor ever would.

Because lust was all it had been. Anger transmuted in the heat of the moment into another far more dangerous passion.

That other girl had hoped some day to fall in love, and to discover the joys of sex in a relationship that mattered, not to give herself unthinkingly on the well-used mattress of a hotel room on a winter afternoon to a man who was, to all intents and purposes, her enemy, whatever his surface attraction.

Because that was nothing less than degrading. And what could she say in her own defence? Plead momentary insanity?

She should have talked to her sister quietly and privately, to warn rather than sit in judgement. Darling Cilla, please—please think what you're doing, because he's not worth it, was what she'd have said. Trying to take care of her as always. Wouldn't she?

Except, I hardly know any more, she thought. And I certainly don't know the creature I became a few hours ago. She was just—a temporary aberration. Something I can't afford.

She sighed, thinking wistfully how wonderful it would be if everyone could put the clock back— just once. Be allowed to correct a truly hideous mistake before any real damage was done.

She collected up her discarded clothes and took them downstairs. She had just filled the washing machine and set it going, when the rear door opened and Mrs Pel, in a warm coat and woollen hat, bustled in on a blast of cold air.

'Why, Miss Ginny,' she exclaimed. 'I wasn't expecting to see you. Did the café close early?'

'No, I—I didn't feel too well, so I came home.' Ginny hoped her flush would be attributed to the warmth of the kitchen rather than telling a downright lie, which was something else she might have to get used to, she acknowledged miserably.

Mrs Pel tutted. 'Lot of nasty viruses about,' she said darkly. 'Now, why don't you go back to bed, and I'll bring you some hot lemon.'

'I think I've spent quite enough time in bed,' said Ginny, her flush deepening as she reverted to perfect truth. 'It would do me more good to take Barney out.'

Mrs Pel looked at her in dismay. 'He's not here, Miss Ginny. A man came for him first thing this morning. Said it was all arranged.'

'Arranged?' Ginny's heart skipped a beat. 'But I knew nothing about it. What's his name?'

'I didn't hear it. Miss Cilla spoke to him. But he seemed pleasant enough—and got Barney into this cage in the back of his Land Rover.'

'A cage?' Ginny was beginning unhappily, fearing the worst, when the front door bell jangled, making Mrs Pel tut again.

'Now who can that be?'

'I've no idea.' *Another lie. Because she knew who it was as surely as if he was standing in front of her.* She went on quickly, 'But Mother and Cilla are out, and I'd really rather not see anyone. So, could you say none of us are here?' She paused. 'Whoever it is.'

'Of course I can.' Mrs Pel regarded her with concern as the bell rang again. 'You do look peaky and no mistake. You run along, and I'll wait till you're safely out of the way.'

Ginny didn't go straight to her room. Instead she

lingered on the galleried landing, shielded from the hall below by an antique cupboard.

She heard Mrs Pel open the door, and say with real pleasure, 'Well, Mr Andre, this is a surprise. But I'm afraid the family are out.'

'Mademoiselle Virginie also?' The query was sharp.

'All of them,' said Mrs Pel stoutly.

There was a silence, then he said quietly, '*Oui, je comprends.*' He paused again. '*À demain,* I have to return to France, Marguerite. Perhaps you would convey my regrets to Madame Charlton for my failure to take my leave of her.' He added drily, 'Although I am sure she will not find it a hardship.'

'Well, I shall miss you, Monsieur Andre. I'm glad to know your mother found the happiness she deserved.' It was Mrs Pel's turn to pause. 'Is there any message you'd like me to pass on—to anyone?'

'Thank you, but no. At the moment, all I can say is—*au revoir.*'

He seemed suddenly to be speaking more loudly but maybe that was Ginny's imagination.

'But please believe,' he went on, 'that I shall be back. And soon.'

From her hiding place, Ginny heard the front

door close and Mrs Pel's footsteps returning to the kitchen.

As she straightened, she realised she was trembling again. Knowing that he hadn't been fooled for a moment. That everything he'd said had been aimed straight at her.

'But when you do return, Monsieur Duchard,' she whispered under her breath, 'you'll find me long gone. And that's a promise.'

CHAPTER SIX

ALTHOUGH MOVING ON was her avowed intention, Ginny hadn't expected Fate to take her quite so literally.

She'd spent a miserable night, almost afraid to go to sleep in case her dreams brought an even more vivid reminder of the afternoon's unbelievable stupidity.

She was fretting, too, over what had happened to Barney. Her mother had categorically denied having any hand in his disappearance while Cilla said merely that the man who'd collected him was 'ordinary' with a name she couldn't remember.

She was tired and depressed when she arrived at work. Twenty minutes later, she was jobless.

'Iris is quite insistent,' Miss Finn said wearily. 'She says you've proved yourself unreliable by walking out in the middle of a busy day without permission and failing to return.

'I said I was sure there was some explanation, but I'm afraid she doesn't want to know.'

'I've just given her the excuse she wanted.' Ginny bent her head. 'And I can't explain either.'

Miss Finn sighed and handed her an envelope. 'You've got two weeks' wages in lieu of notice and I've written you a reference.' She paused. 'Although this might be a good time to consider a change of direction.'

'Yes,' Ginny agreed soberly. 'I—I'd already decided that.'

But in my own time, she thought ruefully, as she departed.

Lost in thought, she was waiting to cross the street when a hand fell on her arm and, to her horror, she found Andre looking grimly down at her.

'*Ou vas tu?*' he demanded. 'I was coming to the café to find you.'

She wrenched free. 'Well, you'd have been unlucky because I've just been fired. And I don't want to be found, so you go your way and I'll go mine.'

His mouth hardened. 'Now you are being ridiculous. There are things that must be said and running away will solve nothing. Now will you walk with me, or must I carry you?'

'Lay one hand on me,' Ginny said hoarsely, 'and I'll scream blue murder.'

'Over a lovers' quarrel? Because that is what I shall say—and be believed.'

'What makes you think so?'

He said softly, 'You have a small crimson mark below your left breast received, I think, at birth. Do you wish the world to know that I kissed it yesterday? *Non? Alors,* come with me now.'

He took her hand firmly in his and led her up the street to the Rose and Crown.

She hung back. Her voice shook a little. 'I—I'm not going back there.'

'*Qu'as tu?*' He stared at her, then gave a short laugh. '*Mon Dieu,* you think I have time for such things? We are going to talk.'

He took her into the hotel's deserted dining room and, when a surprised waitress appeared, ordered coffee.

Once they'd been served and were alone again, he said abruptly, 'Why did you not tell me you were a virgin? It was something I needed to know. And do not deny it,' he added swiftly. 'You bled a little.'

Ginny's colour mounted. 'I didn't realise. Anyway, it doesn't matter.'

Slowly, Andre stirred the light brown liquid in

his cup. 'I used no protection, *ma mie,* so it could matter a great deal. *Tu comprends?*'

Ginny stared at him, wondering why he seemed to have receded to some far distance. She said huskily, 'I understand—but I don't believe it.'

The dark brows lifted. 'You do not believe how babies are made?'

'No,' she said hotly. 'I mean it's not that easy to get pregnant. People try for years—take fertility drugs. Do IVF. It can't possibly have happened just like that on—on my first time.'

His mouth twisted. 'But for many millions, *ma belle,* it does happen every day—just like that. And you may be one of them. For which I blame myself *entièrement.* I should have known how innocent you truly were and taken adequate precautions.'

She looked down at the table. She said in a voice she didn't recognise, 'And my sister?'

'You concern yourself unduly.' He shrugged. 'She knows very well how to protect herself. One would not think she was the younger.'

She gasped. 'Is—is that all you have to say?'

'For the moment, yes.' He paused. 'As for you, Virginie, it is time to think only about yourself and the child we may have made.'

She swallowed. 'Well, if it's happened, it's

my problem, not yours. And if necessary I'll deal with it.'

'And how will that be?' There was a note in his voice which made her shiver. 'A few hours in some *clinique* and the baby will be gone, as if it had never existed. You think you can do that?'

She looked down again. 'If I have to.'

'And I say you cannot,' Andre told her harshly. 'That for you, at least, such a thing could never be forgotten and you would regret it for the rest of your life.'

She made herself meet his gaze. Spoke icily. 'Not my only regret, believe me.'

He made a slight cynical bow. 'At least we can agree on that. But we cannot change the past, only deal with the present. And the future.'

'I can manage that for myself,' she flashed.

'*Vraiment?* I doubt that. You have lost your job and may soon be homeless, unless you hope to join your mother at the cottage.' He watched her colour deepen and nodded. '*Eh, bien,* I have another plan. You heard me say I am returning to France? Come with me.'

The breath caught in her throat. When she could speak: 'That's ridiculous. You must be quite mad.'

He smiled faintly. 'Sometimes, I think so too, but

not now. You have a passport. You know where to find your birth certificate? Because you will need it.'

'What for?'

'For the legal formalities,' he said. 'Before we can be married.'

There was a silence, then she said unsteadily, 'Now I know you're crazy. Because I would never marry you. Not if...' And hesitated.

'If I were the last man on earth?' he asked drily. '*Merci du compliment.*' He paused. 'Virginie, it is not easy to be a single mother. If my own mother still lived, she would tell you so and that she was thankful to be offered a home and the protection of a man's name. I offer you the same.'

'It's impossible,' she said stormily. 'For one thing, we're practically strangers.'

'Hardly that.' He had the gall to sound faintly amused. 'After yesterday.'

'That was no wish of mine,' she flared in return.

There was another silence, then: 'Forgive me,' he said, too courteously. 'I am a little confused. Are you saying that I took you against your will?'

Ginny bit her lip. 'Well—no. Not exactly.'

'I am relieved to hear it.' His tone was harsh.

'But it changes nothing,' she went on quickly.

'Marriage is out of the question, particularly when we don't know if I am pregnant.'

'Then until we can be sure, I will make you a different offer,' he said. 'A roof over your head and paid employment.'

'As what?'

'Not what you are so clearly imagining.' His retort was brusque. 'I have never yet paid a woman to share my bed and you, *ma mie,* will not be the first.

'I have heard from my father how much you contributed to the running of his household,' he went on. *'Alors,* a solution presents itself.'

'You want me to be your housekeeper? I wouldn't dream of such a thing.'

He pushed away his untouched coffee and sat back, regarding her thoughtfully. 'The time for dreaming is past, Virginie, and you must face reality. What is your own plan for the future?'

'To find a permanent and worthwhile job,' she said defiantly. 'I might even go back to London.'

'To *ta marraine?* Your godmother?'

She shook her head. 'She and my mother quarrelled, so we've lost touch.'

'But you have other friends there?'

'No,' she said. 'Not that it's anything to do with you.'

'It is very much my concern. A city like London is no place for a girl without work, family or connections.' He was silent for a moment, drumming his fingers restlessly on the table. He said abruptly, 'I will make you another offer. Come with me to Burgundy until you know whether or not you are *enceinte.* If you are not, I will give you the money to return to England and support you while you train for whatever profession you desire.'

She said slowly, 'You would do that. But why?'

'Because I believe it is what my father would have wished. What he himself would have done had he lived.'

'You make it very hard for me to refuse.'

'Then why do so?'

'Because there's another side to the coin. If I am pregnant, I still won't want to stay. To be married. To you.'

'And you think I will force you?' He shrugged. 'Marriage in France, Virginie, is hedged about with respectability and performed in front of the Mayor. The ceremony would not take place if it was thought you were unwilling.'

He paused, then added levelly, '*D'ailleurs,* by that time you may come to see that, for the child's sake, becoming my wife is your only rational course.'

My first, perhaps only, proposal of marriage, thought Ginny, pain twisting inside her, and it's happening in a dismal room smelling of Full English Breakfasts, and with nothing but rationality and business deals on offer.

She said quietly, 'I can't promise that. And I'd like some time on my own—to think.'

'To think or to run away?'

'To decide.' She pushed back her chair and rose. 'Perhaps, Monsieur Duchard, it's time we began to trust each other, if you want your plans to succeed.'

He got to his feet too. 'And I would feel more optimistic, *mademoiselle,* if you were to call me Andre.' He added gently, 'Under the circumstances, such continued formality between us is nonsense.'

Her swift flush was painful. 'I suppose so.'

He added briskly, '*En tout cas,* I require your answer now if we are to catch the afternoon flight to Dijon.'

She took a deep breath, her stomach churning as a voice in her head told her that his proposition was ludicrous—impossible. Something she should not contemplate. For all sorts of reasons.

The feel of his skin against hers. Oh God, the taste of him...

And heard herself say shakily, 'Then—yes, I agree.' She paused. 'On one condition. That you treat me as an employee. Give me my own space.'

He nodded, his face cool and unsmiling. '*Soit.* Let it be as you wish.' He added, 'I will come for you at noon. Pack your warmest clothing only—and not the hideous dress, *hein?*'

Her gasp of indignation followed him to the door—and this time she had no desire to laugh.

On her way home, she called at the bank and drew out what little money she possessed, leaving just enough to keep the account open. This, plus her wages, gave her at least a semblance of independence.

She'd hoped to have the house to herself, but she could hear Rosina and Cilla laughing and talking in the drawing room, so taking a deep breath she walked in—on chaos.

The floor was littered with empty carrier bags and tissue paper, and their contents, mostly beach and cocktail wear was strewn across one of the sofas.

'Virginia.' Rosina sounded faintly defensive. 'Why are you home at this hour?'

'I've been fired.' She gestured around her. 'What's this?'

'Some holiday things. After all this stress, I decided I needed a break, and Cilla and I have managed to get a last-minute deal in the Seychelles, so we popped into Lanchester to do some shopping.'

Ginny turned to her sister. 'Is Jonathan going to be happy about this?'

Cilla shrugged. 'If not, it serves him right. He's been so difficult lately.'

'And if you're no longer at that dreary little café, you can look after things here,' Rosina chimed in brightly.

'Except I shan't be here either,' Ginny said quietly. 'Andre Duchard has offered me a temporary job in France while I consider my future.'

There was an ominous silence. When Rosina spoke, her voice was steel. 'If this is a joke, it's not amusing.'

'I'm perfectly serious. We'll be leaving in about forty minutes and I've come home to pack.'

'You—and that man? I can't believe even you would stoop so low.' Rosina flung out a dramatic arm. 'Oh, I shall never forgive you for this—you little Judas.'

'But at least I shan't be a drain on your resources, Mother.' Ginny lifted her chin, trying not to see Cilla's expression of frozen resentment and disbelief. 'You can't have it all ways.'

She paused. 'And maybe some of our problems stem from other causes,' she added, and walked out, closing the door on another furious tirade.

Packing did not take long, her clothes and other personal possessions barely filling the suitcase she hadn't used since boarding school.

Not much to show for nearly twenty-two years, she thought wryly, as she added the framed photograph of Andrew with Barney that she'd taken from the desk in the study. Something, she told herself, that only she would value.

As she carried her case downstairs, Mrs Pel suddenly appeared, her face troubled. 'So you're really leaving, Miss Ginny? And your mother beside herself, saying things about you and Mr Andre that don't bear repeating. Are you quite sure you know what you're doing, my dear?'

Ginny tried to smile. 'I thought you'd be pleased. After all, Mrs Pel, you were the one who told me to spread my wings and fly.'

'Yes,' Mrs Pel said soberly. 'But only for the right reasons.'

Ginny put down her case and hugged her. 'I'll make them right,' she said, more cheerfully than she felt. 'And I won't be gone for ever. I'll write to you at Market Lane.' She hesitated. 'And if there's any news of Barney, can you let me know?'

'Of course.' Mrs Pel sighed. 'But I'll be glad to be gone, and that's the truth. This house will never be the same again.'

What will? Ginny asked herself tautly as the hall clock began to strike twelve, and she heard the sound of a car approaching up the drive.

Head held high, she walked out, closing the door behind her.

Once the plane had taken off and she knew there was no turning back, she sat stiffly, hands gripped together in her lap, only too aware of the intimacy imposed by the seating, the proximity of Andre's thigh to hers. Fighting the memories it aroused. Dreading the inevitable conversation.

But Andre said very little. After making sure she was warm enough and ordering coffee, he occupied himself with a sheaf of papers he'd taken from the leather satchel she recalled from their first meeting.

All too soon they were landing at Dijon, where a stocky young man, introduced to Ginny as Jules Rameau, was waiting with a battered Range Rover to take them to Terauze.

Slumped in the back, unable to understand the quick-fire exchanges between the two in the front, Ginny found herself swamped by weariness mingled with depression.

The quarrel with her mother had been inevitable, but she still regretted it. When she returned to England, she would have to find a way to make peace with Cilla too. Perhaps a week or two on a sun-drenched island would make both of them more amenable to reason.

And maybe pigs would fly...

The jolting of the Range Rover as it slowed, then halted, dragged her back to the here and now. That, and the piercing cold of the night air as she left the car.

There were cobbles underfoot and she stumbled slightly, only to find Andre's steadying hand under her elbow as they moved towards a lighted doorway.

They walked along a flagged passage and through another door into the kitchen beyond, and Ginny stood for a moment, feeling a blissful warmth surround her. Aware, too, of an equally heavenly aroma from a cast-iron pot on the big stove.

Her gaze travelled from the wide fireplace where logs smouldered and the wooden rocking chair next to it, to the dresser filling an entire wall, its shelves groaning with china and glassware, and on up to the beamed ceiling where strings of onions and bunches of dried herbs hung from hooks.

Through an archway, she could see the gleam of a sink and the shining white of a large washing machine and tumble dryer.

By the time she left, she thought, all this would be totally familiar. But right now, she felt as if she'd landed on a different planet, and she was scared—especially about what tonight might bring.

He said he'd leave me alone, she reminded herself. But how do I know he'll keep his word—about anything?

Andre's voice broke into her reverie. 'I regret that my father is not here to welcome you, but he is in Paris until tomorrow.'

He was briskly ridding himself of his coat and,

after a slight hesitation, Ginny did the same, before joining him at the long table covered in oil-cloth and set with cutlery and a platter of bread, and watching as Jules ladled stew into bowls and Andre filled glasses from the unmarked bottle of red wine in the centre of the table.

'*Boeuf bourguignon,*' he said, handing her a bowl. Taking a seat opposite, he raised his glass to her. '*Salut.* And welcome to Burgundy.'

Tired as she was, Ginny did not miss the faintly caustic glance directed at him by Jules as he joined them. Maybe her arrival was not going to be greeted by universal rejoicing, and Andre might possibly come to regret his hasty offer.

She'd thought she'd be too tired to eat, but it took just one delicious mouthful of tender beef, beautifully cooked with wine, herbs, tiny onions and mushrooms to convince her she was wrong.

The wine was astonishing too, filling her mouth with rich earthy flavours while caressing her throat like velvet. Or a lover's touch...

She even had some of the sharp, creamy cheese which followed the stew and sighed as she finally pushed her plate away.

'That was—utterly delicious,' she said stiltedly

and looked at Jules. 'My compliments to the chef, *monsieur.*'

For a moment he stared at her, astounded, then a broad grin spread across his rugged face as he turned to Andre, making some incomprehensible remark.

'Jules is flattered,' Andre translated. 'But the credit must go to his aunt, who has been cook here for many years. Madame Rameau is busy elsewhere tonight, but you will meet her tomorrow.'

Jules got to his feet, still grinning. He said, *'Bonne nuit,* Andre, *mam'selle.'* His dark eyes danced as he looked from one to the other. *'Et dormez bien, n'est ce pas?'*

Well, she didn't need a translation of that, Ginny thought, flushing angrily as Jules sauntered across the kitchen and out into the night.

She said tautly, 'Where has he gone?'

'Home to sleep. He lives in a house on the edge of the vineyard. La Petite Maison is always occupied by the manager.'

He picked up her coat and suitcase. 'And I think it is time that you, too, Virginie, went to bed. *Viens avec moi.*'

A door in the corner led up a winding flight of wooden stairs to a curtained archway. He held the velvet aside to allow her to precede him and she stepped through to find herself in a broad corridor, its pastel walls illumined by elegant gilded sconces, which appeared to lead to a pair of ornate double doors at the end.

Conscious that with Jules' departure, she seemed to be here alone with him, she felt her apprehension mounting.

Swallowing, she saw he'd reached the doors and was holding one of them open, motioning her to enter. Ginny obeyed warily and stopped dead, gasping, as she gazed round the biggest bedroom she'd ever seen.

All the elaborately carved furniture—the enormous *armoire*, the dressing table and chair, the night tables and the linen chest at the foot of the bed—were clearly very old and made from wood the colour of horse chestnuts. While the bed itself...

It was easily more than double the width of the queen-size bed she'd slept in at Barrowdean, making it what? Emperor-size? Dictator-of-the-world-size? And rendered even more imposing by its four carved posts, and its canopy and curtains in pale gold brocade.

And totally inappropriate for single occupation—if that had ever been his intention.

Her heartbeat faltered then steadied as Andre set her coat and case down on the chest, then walked across the room to open a door on the other side and reveal the gleam of ivory tiles.

'I am sure Clothilde has provided all that you need,' he said. 'Permit me to wish you goodnight.'

As he reached the bedroom door, she said huskily, 'Just a moment. There must be some mistake. This is not a servant's room.'

'*Tu as raison,*' he agreed. 'This is the room always occupied by the Baron de Terauze and his wife. Papa Bertrand, being a widower, chooses to sleep elsewhere. And although I am not yet the Baron or a husband, I have decided you will sleep here as my chosen bride until I am legally entitled to join you.' His smile touched her like the stroke of a hand across her skin. 'I live for that night, *ma belle.*'

Her throat tightened. She said dazedly, 'But that's tantamount to a public announcement. You can't do that.'

He shrugged. 'Nevertheless, it is done.'

She gave him a challenging look. 'And when it's

confirmed that there is no baby and I go back to England, what will you do then?'

'I shall cross that bridge,' he said softly, 'only if I come to it.'

'When,' she said. 'Not—if. And another thing. You told us all—you let us think you worked in a vineyard.'

'And so I do,' he said. 'Very hard, and so do Papa Bertrand and Jules. If your mother wished to believe that as well as a bastard I was a peasant toiling in a field, that was her concern.' He added reflectively, 'But I do not think, Virginie, that you were fooled even for a moment.'

Her skin warmed as she remembered with blazing clarity that strange shock of recognition when she opened the door to him and—later—the exquisitely practised sophistication of his lovemaking.

She said, 'I think it was a lousy trick to play.'

'*Vraiment?*' His smile was edged. 'I thought it would please you, *ma mie,* to find that you also will not be required to live in a hovel.'

'You're wrong,' she said shakily. 'Nothing about this—arrangement pleases me, or ever will.'

His mouth hardened. 'Then let us hope a night's rest will bring you to a more equable state of mind. Because this is my future as well as yours, and you

would do well to accept it as I am prepared to do.'
He inclined his head curtly. '*À demain.*'

For a moment, Ginny stood staring at the door
he had closed behind him and then, with a little
inarticulate cry, she ran to it, twisting the heavy
key in the lock. Wanting the physical bulk of wood
and iron to create a barrier between them.

And ashamed to her soul that she should feel it
necessary.

CHAPTER SEVEN

GINNY AWOKE SLOWLY, as if she was swimming upwards through layer after languid layer of comfort.

For a moment, as she opened her eyes, she felt disorientated, looking round an unfamiliar room from the depths of an unfamiliar bed. But then the memories of yesterday's incredible sequence of events came flooding back.

She had not expected to sleep and yet it seemed she had—almost as soon as the silk-shaded bedside lamp had been extinguished.

Off with the light, then out like a light, she thought, her mouth twisting. But it's a new day now and I need to be wide awake and firing on all cylinders to deal with whatever it brings.

She pushed aside the covers and slid down to the floor, the polished boards striking cold to her feet. She retrieved her ruby robe from her case and huddled it on over her pyjamas before going to the window and opening the shutters. To find herself standing motionless, gasping at the unexpected glory confronting her.

There had been a hard frost in the night, and, as a result, the red-gold ball of the early sun had turned the vine-clad slopes spreading as far as the eye could see into living flame.

A welcome contrast to the darkness of her arrival and maybe, from now on, she would see more clearly in other ways.

But maybe not hear or speak so well, with only her schoolgirl French to rely on. But that would probably be the least of her inadequacies, she thought, pulling her robe further around her with a shiver and taking one last look at the vibrant glow of the landscape before turning away.

She picked a pair of jeans and a thick navy Guernsey from her case, then transferred the rest of her meagre haul of clothing to the depths of the *armoire* where it looked small and slightly lost. Rather how I feel myself, she thought wryly, locating her hairdryer and putting it on the bed.

Collecting a handful of underwear and a towel, she was on her way to the bathroom when there was a loud knock at the bedroom door and a rattle as the handle was tried.

She halted. 'Who is it?' Just as if she didn't know.

'Andre.' He rattled the handle again. 'Open the door, Virginie.'

Reluctantly, she obeyed, turning the key in the lock. He walked in and stood, hands on hips, his face grim as he looked her up and down. Although she was perfectly decent, Ginny had to fight an impulse to draw her robe even more closely round her.

Which was ridiculous when he knew perfectly well what she looked like naked, she thought with a pang that mingled embarrassed discomfort with something altogether more ambiguous.

'I thought we had agreed to trust one another,' he commented coldly. 'So why lock your door?'

She shrugged defensively. 'My first night in a strange house. I felt—nervous.' And she was nervous now. His arrival made the room seem almost smaller. And he hadn't shaved, rekindling unwanted memories of the way his stubble had grazed her bare skin.

He nodded. 'And if there had been a fire and we had been unable to reach you? What then?'

'Is that likely?'

'No,' he said. 'But not impossible. *Alors...*' He took the key from the lock and slipped it into the pocket of his jeans. 'I came to say that Madame

Rameau will be preparing breakfast. I hope you will join us.'

'Yes,' she said jerkily. 'Yes, of course. I—I'll soon be ready.'

He turned towards the door, then swung back and came over to her, his fingers reaching for her sleeve, grasping the soft ruby fabric. He said softly, 'I find I do not care for this garment. Something else I should have told you to leave behind, *ma mie.*'

And, before she could form any kind of protest, went.

High-handed, dictatorial, and arrogant were just some of the words Ginny muttered under her breath as she stood under the blissful heat of the powerful shower. Words that she repeated over and over again as if they were a spell which would give her some kind of protection.

Although she should not need protection. She was hardly here through choice, yet while she might have accepted the deal on offer, there were still parameters to be drawn. Limits to be observed.

Her mood was not improved when she realised she could not plug in her hairdryer, and therefore she would be going down to breakfast with her hair hanging to her shoulders in rats' tails.

But what the hell, she thought, raking the damp strands back from her face. Looking attractive was hardly a preferred option.

She took off her robe and, shivering in bra and briefs, reached for her jeans. At which moment the door opened and Andre walked in.

She snatched up the jeans and held them defensively in front of her. Her voice shook. 'Can't you knock?'

He shrugged. 'I have seen you wearing less.'

'I don't need any reminder of that.' She lifted her chin. 'What do you want?'

'I thought you would need this.' He tossed an adapter plug on to the bed beside the dryer. 'I do not wish you to add a bout of pneumonia to the list of grievances against me you are undoubtedly preparing.'

'Thank you.' She bit her lip. 'That was—thoughtful.'

His brows lifted in faint amusement. 'You said that, *chérie,* as if you were chewing broken glass,' he observed. 'I had hoped you would be more grateful.' He paused. 'I would welcome as little as a smile.'

She said in a low voice, 'Perhaps I haven't much

to smile about. And on the subject of pneumonia, I'd like to get dressed in peace.'

'*Hélas,* I can only offer privacy,' he said sardonically, his eyes travelling over her in frank and unhurried reminiscence. 'Peace, *ma mie,* is a very different matter.' And added, 'For both of us.'

It wasn't until the door closed behind him that Ginny realised she was holding her breath.

She fumbled her way into her clothing with hands that shook, but the necessity of wielding dryer and brush to restore her hair to its usual shining curtain gave her a modicum of composure.

Making her way downstairs, she paused at the kitchen door, silently rehearsing an apology for being late, then marched in only to find that preparations for breakfast had apparently not yet begun.

Instead she was immediately conscious of an odd tension in the silent room as if her arrival had halted a conversation, she thought as she registered the woman standing by the fireplace.

She was tall with silver-grey hair cut in a sleek angular bob and a striking, even beautiful face, and Ginny found herself struggling to make a connection between the newcomer and Jules with his distinctly sturdy build and blunt, slightly pugnacious features.

She summoned a smile and walked across the room, ready to shake hands. '*Bonjour,* Madame Rameau? *Comment allez vous? Je suis* Virginia Mason.'

'Madame Rameau,' the other woman repeated wonderingly. Adding in English, 'Is this perhaps a joke?'

'*Au contraire,* it is a mistake on my part, Monique.' Andre, standing with Jules at the window, spoke coolly. 'We were not anticipating the pleasure of seeing you at this hour and Mademoiselle Mason was expecting to meet Clothilde.' He came forward to Ginny's side. 'Virginie, allow me to introduce Mademoiselle Chaloux.'

The other woman smiled, showing perfect teeth. 'And Clothilde, *naturellement,* is late. Occupied with some little medical emergency, no doubt. But it is an unexpected pleasure to find Mademoiselle Mason among us. I had assumed...' She broke off, her smile widening. 'But enough of that. I shall now look forward to practising my English as I once did with your dear mother, Andre.'

Ginny said politely, 'I don't think you need practice, *mademoiselle.*'

'How charming of you to say so.' Mademoiselle Chaloux turned to Andre. 'I have called, *mon cher,* to say that Bertrand expects to be here by late afternoon.'

'That is good of you, Monique,' Andre said courteously. 'But he informed me of that himself last night.'

'Ah,' she said lightly. 'Then I need not have delayed my start to the day.' She nodded in Ginny's direction. '*Au revoir, mademoiselle.* We shall meet again very soon. This evening at dinner, perhaps.'

'*Non, hélas.*' Andre's tone expressed polite regret. 'Tonight we plan to dine *en famille,* in order to welcome Mademoiselle Mason. I am sure you understand.'

There was the slightest pause, then: 'But, of course.'

Another glinting smile around the room and she was gone.

Ginny heard Jules mutter something inaudible and with that came an almost perceptible relaxation in the atmosphere.

So I wasn't imagining things, she thought. She drew a breath.

'I'm sorry I made that mistake over the names. I hope Mademoiselle Chaloux isn't too upset.'

'*Ça ne fait rien.*' Andre shrugged. 'Between Clothilde and herself there has always been friction, for many reasons. Monique's father was the doctor here for some years, and she acted as his receptionist and secretary. He believed in orthodox medicine and hospital births for all mothers.

'Clothilde, *par contraste,* is the unofficial village midwife, delivering babies at home in their parents' beds and brewing medicine from herbs in her kitchen, and many people turn first to her.'

Jules said grimly, 'In past centuries, *sans doute, la famille* Chaloux would have denounced my aunt as a witch.'

Andre's mouth relaxed into a grin that made Ginny's heartbeat quicken ridiculously. 'For myself, I wonder what Clothilde would have called Monique.'

She tried to speak lightly. 'She sounds quite something.'

'Judge for yourself,' he said as a door banged and an instant later a woman surged into the room, talking nineteen to the dozen, with a canvas bag in one hand and several baguettes under her other arm.

The antithesis of Mademoiselle Chaloux, the newcomer was short, clad in a cape like a small tent, her rosy double-chinned face crowned by an untidy topknot of pepper and salt hair. The removal of the cape revealed that she was built on generous lines, full-bosomed and wide-hipped, her ample body supported on sturdy legs in red woollen tights.

As she paused for breath, lively brown eyes discovered Ginny and narrowed. 'So she is here—the daughter of *Monsieur ton père?*'

'*Sa belle fille.* His stepdaughter,' Andre corrected with faint emphasis.

She sent him a shrewd glance, the small mouth pursing, then looked back at Ginny, examining her slowly from head to toe. She gave a brisk nod. '*Soyez bien-venue, petite. Asseyez-vous.*'

In next to no time, breakfast was on the table with bread and croissants still warm from the bakery, a choice of peach or cherry jam and *café au lait* served in cups like bowls.

As she ate, Ginny found herself watching Andre under her lashes, seeing him for the first time on his own territory. Listening to the ebb and flow of his conversation with Jules, the turn of his head, the movement of his hands to stress a point. Everything about him leaving no doubt as to who was the boss here.

And her boss too, she supposed without pleasure as she finished her coffee, then watched, astonished as Madame Rameau began to empty the canvas bag, unloading a *patisserie* box followed by potatoes, onions, a cabbage, a bunch of carrots and a large chicken together with several jars and containers.

She said, 'Well, dinner looks good.'

Andre grinned. 'Except that it is lunch. Dinner will be another affair altogether.'

She closed her eyes. 'My God.'

Jules had already left and as Andre drained the last of his coffee and rose, Ginny leaned across the table. She said quietly, 'I came here to work. Perhaps you'd explain my duties so I can start.'

'*Eh bien,*' he said. 'You may begin by coming for a walk with me. I wish to show you the vineyard.'

She hesitated and he added softly, '*S'il te plaît,* Virginie. Please.'

She was chagrined to feel herself blush and didn't know whether to blame the coaxing note in his voice or the fact that Madame Rameau was regarding them benignly, hands on hips.

She got up from the table. 'I'll fetch my coat.'

He held out a detaining hand. 'But before we go, you may wish to telephone your mother to tell her you have arrived and are safe.'

'I already did so,' she said. 'The machine picked up my message.'

'She has not returned the call.'

'I doubt she'll want to.' Ginny looked away, biting her lip. 'We—we parted on bad terms.'

'Ah,' he said and paused. 'But at least give her the chance to do so, *ma mie,* or you may regret it.'

'You sound almost sorry for her,' she challenged. 'What's brought about this change?'

His voice was quiet. 'I would feel sorry for anyone who has turned away the gift of happiness.'

And what was she supposed to make of that? Ginny wondered as she sat on the edge of her bed to pull on her boots before zipping herself into her quilted coat.

Outside, it was cold and crisp, the sun now a pale globe in the misty winter sky. They left by the rear door, crossing a walled courtyard with empty stone troughs waiting for spring blooms.

Beyond its double wrought-iron gates the vines were also waiting, no longer invisible in the early morning dazzle, but stretching, rank upon rank of them, as far as the eye could see, and planted, Ginny saw, with almost military precision against the neat lines of wooden posts and wire which supported them, in broad alternating bands of grass and ploughed tan soil.

She paused halfway up the slope, drawing a sharp breath and Andre looked down at her and smiled.

'You are surprised.'

'Well—yes. I didn't expect it to be so neat and orderly.'

He nodded. 'As my father said—like his office desk.'

She realised that Andrew must have stood here, maybe on this very spot, taking in this very different world. Perhaps formulating the decisions that had led to these tumultuous repercussions in her own life.

She spoke quickly, fighting the sudden tightening of her throat. 'I—I didn't think it would be so big either.'

'We have over thirty acres, this area planted with Pinot Noir, the grape that is Burgundy's jewel. From it we produce our Grand Cru Baron Emile, our most valuable wine.'

'Is that what we had last night?'

He laughed. '*Non, hélas.* That was our Bourgogne Villages, although that is also highly regarded, especially by the region's restaurateurs.'

He pointed. 'And over there, where you see that wall, we grow the Chardonnay grapes for our white wine, Clos Sainte Marie de Terauze. But I do not expect you to walk that far,' he added as they resumed their climb, their boots crunching over the frosty grass.

'Or remember all the information either, I hope.' She sent him a defiant look, suppressing all the other questions that, to her own surprise, she actually wanted to ask, not least about the dynamics back at the house.

At the same time she found herself registering the almost proprietorial note in his voice. A man who loves his work, she thought, and she could hardly blame him for that.

She went on quickly, 'Andrew may have bought into this haven of rural tranquillity and charm, but please don't expect me to do the same.'

His brows lifted. 'Terauze may be charming but it is rarely tranquil. Making a wonderful vintage is hard work with great risk. It is not easy to work in harmony with nature, when nature so often resists. My father came to understand this. To wish to be part of it.'

He paused. 'And he intended you to accompany him here to share in it too.'

She gasped. 'To live here? You mean—with Mother and Cilla?'

'*Non.* He knew they would never agree to his plan, so he made other arrangements for them, as you have seen.'

She said hoarsely, 'And he thought I would just—walk away and leave them? I don't believe it.'

'He felt, *peut-être,* that they did not deserve such loyalty.' He allowed her to absorb that then added, 'He wanted to show you that there were other possibilities in this world, *ma mie.* A different way of living.'

'Well, this will never be mine,' Ginny said stonily, her clenched fists buried deep in her pockets. 'Nor do I believe that I'm going to be punished for the rest of my life for one stupid, ghastly mistake.'

'Is that how you remember it? Because I do not. It was certainly not wise —but ghastly?' He shook his head slowly. 'Never that.'

Ginny looked away from the sudden caress in his gaze, aware of an unwelcome churning in the pit of her stomach at the memories it sparked. 'It makes no difference. As soon as I know there's no reason for me to stay, I shall be out of here and on my way home, as we agreed.'

'And what home is that?' He sounded politely interested.

'I'll find one.' She lifted her chin. 'Because, even if you break our agreement, I shall still leave. Whatever you think, I can find work and—and fend for myself. I'm not like my sister.'

He frowned. 'I think you do her an injustice,' he said quietly. 'She has never had a chance to prove herself—or been required to do so.'

'Then it's a great pity you didn't bring her here instead of me,' she flashed.

He shrugged. 'She would have refused. She prefers the safety of an idle marriage to the rich Monsieur Welburn.'

'But you're rich now, thanks to Andrew. You could have offered her the same.' Her voice was suddenly husky. 'She—clearly found you more than attractive.'

'Like most pretty girls, she likes to flirt,' he said sardonically. '*Alors,* I doubt she would find working beside me each day, sharing my bed at night and raising our children quite so appealing.'

Pain twisted inside her as if someone had inserted a small, thin knife between her ribs. She said stiffly, 'Well, when all this is over, and I'm gone, you can look for someone willing to fit into your cosy little plan —if such a person exists.'

'*Pas de problème,*' he said softly. 'As you say, I am a rich man, and one must be a realist about these things.' He smiled at her. '*D'ailleurs,* it may not be necessary. Our agreement works in two ways, so perhaps, *après tout,* you will not be leaving.'

'Please don't count on it.' They had reached the top of the incline, and paused, facing each other, their breath mingling in the chill air. Anger and other less definable emotions crisped her tone. 'Thank you for the tour, but I have to tell you that one vine looks very like another to me. I'd like to go back now.'

'If you wish,' he said. 'Although there is one last thing I brought you here to see.'

She looked at the undulating landscape with its regiments of vines, her brows lifting. 'You mean I've missed something? I can hardly wait.'

'Sarcasm does not become you.' He took her by the shoulders and she stiffened, panic rising inside her. Because she could not let him touch her. She dared not...

But instead of pulling her towards him, Andre turned her to face the way they had come, and she saw behind them, sheltered like a jewel by the wooded hills behind it, a broad and stately rectangle of grey stone, its roof tiled in faded red, and a tower like a tall pepperpot at each corner.

She drew a startled breath. 'My God, it's not just a house, it's a castle. Like something from a fairy tale.'

'The Château Terauze,' he said quietly. 'I wished you to see it for the first time from this spot.'

She gestured around her. 'So as well as being Andrew's heir, you're due to inherit all this too.'

'*Mais oui,* but not, I hope, for many years to come. Papa Bertrand is well and strong.'

She said, 'Does he—your adoptive father—know about me?'

'*Bien sûr.* He heard a great deal from Andrew.'

'Andrew talked about me—here, and to him?'

She looked away. 'All this was going on—and I didn't have the slightest idea.' She gave a brief shaken laugh. 'Unbelievable.' She paused. 'How did he and Monsieur Duchard become such friends?'

'You mean when they were both in love with the same woman?'

Andre's mouth twisted. 'And the answer is—very slowly. Even as a child, I could recognise the awkwardness in my father's visits. See that my mother found them difficult, at times almost unbearable.'

'Then why did she allow them?'

'Her sense of honour demanded it. She would accept no money from him, but she agreed he had a right to see his child. Also, she was grateful that he had not opposed Bertrand's wish to adopt me after their marriage.'

She said slowly, 'It sounds a terrible situation. But what I don't understand is why she chose to come here at all.'

'She had a friend here in Terauze who had been her *correspondante* from their school days.' He paused. 'A penfriend, you would say. There had been visits on both sides, but Maman loved it here and came several times after leaving school to stay with her friend and help with the grape-picking, looking on it as her second home.

'*Alors,* when she needed help, she came here to find a refuge where she could think calmly and without pressure about her future and that of her child.'

Ginny bit her lip. 'In which case, history seems to be repeating itself.'

'*Au contraire.* You have not come to find yourself alone. My mother was not so fortunate. She discovered that, over a year before, her friend had moved away to Provence with her family, leaving no address.'

Ginny gasped. 'What did she do?'

'She could afford a room at the *auberge* for a night or two, but on the way she felt suddenly faint and sat down on the church steps to recover. Papa Bertrand was passing in his car, recognised her, and insisted on bringing her back to the Château.'

'You mean he remembered her from her grape-picking days?'

Andre smiled. 'Ah, more than that. They knew each other well. As a child, he teased her. As a girl, he fell in love with her. And when she came back as a woman, he was determined to make her his wife, and raise her child as his own.' He paused. 'But she was not easy to persuade. Not least because his father, who had other ideas for him, opposed his plans.'

'And she didn't wish to cause trouble in his family.' Ginny sighed. 'I can understand that.'

'So he moved out of the *château* to La Petite Maison, where I was born. But, sadly, his father refused to accept the marriage until the day he died.

'And for a long time, my mother did not wish

to move to the château, because of the unhappy memories it held for her.'

The fairy tale had its dark side, Ginny thought, glancing back at the château with a quick shiver.

Which he noticed. 'You are cold? We will go back to the house.' Adding quietly, 'But not quite yet.'

Before she realised his intention, he turned her to face him, pulling her into his arms and pinning her against him, while his mouth sought hers.

Sky and earth were tilting dizzily as her senses leapt at the pressure of his lean, hard body, the stark insistence of his lips parting hers in a kiss that she could not withstand. A kiss that she ached for and which made her realise in one devastating moment that if he was to pull her down with him to the frosty ground, she would not be able to resist him. Nor, to her eternal shame, would she want to.

But even as she felt herself melting into surrender, Andre released her and stepped back as if nothing particular had happened.

Her voice not entirely under her control, she said, 'What the hell was all that about?'

'Let us call it—a welcome to my world.'

'Your world.' She could feel the thud of her heart

against her ribs as she challenged his gaze. 'But not mine. Never in a thousand years.'

She turned and started down the slope, resisting an almost overwhelming impulse to run, as the sudden tightening of her throat muscles warned her that tears were not far away. A self-betrayal she knew she could not afford.

Not then, she told herself, or at any time until she had left Terauze behind her for good.

CHAPTER EIGHT

ON GINNY'S RETURN, the kitchen was already beginning to fill with the enticing aroma of chicken and vegetables cooking slowly in another big pot on the stove, but she did not linger, but hurried to her room to discard her coat and boots, trying without success to dismiss from her mind that blinding, agonising moment of desire that had devastated her defences against him only a few moments before.

She should have fought him off, she told herself angrily. She'd been mad to expose herself to such danger. Even crazier to try and pretend the danger did not exist.

It had been a shock to discover that Andrew had planned to live at the château.

And I, she thought, swallowing, I would have lived here too—if I'd agreed to come with him—which, of course, I wouldn't have done. But, if I had, Andre and I would have met under totally different circumstances…

But I won't think about that, she told herself sternly, aware that for a moment her mind had gone into a curious kind of freefall. I'll deal with things as they are.

She had just hung away her coat, when there was a sharp rap on the door, and Andre came in, his face set and unsmiling.

He said, 'Have you spoken yet to your mother?'

'There's still no answer. I'll try again later.'

'You will be wasting your time,' he said. 'Monsieur Hargreaves is also trying to find her. He wishes to arrange for Barrowdean to be cleared for the new tenants. Yet he has learned that she has flown out to the Seychelles to take a holiday with your sister, and cannot be contacted.'

He paused. 'You knew of this plan?'

Ginny bit her lip. 'Well, yes, but I had no idea she meant to leave so soon.' *Or, more worryingly, leave no details of her trip.*

He frowned. 'I find her decision curious. Does she fully understand the terms of my father's will—its financial implications for her?'

'I think so.' Ginny flushed. 'But you also have to understand how stressful everything has been for her—losing Andrew and—all that's followed.' *Including my decision to come here...*

'She was probably too desperate for an interlude away from it all to consider the cost.'

'Then she must learn to do so,' he said drily.

He paused again, his eyes studying her, travelling from the startled, vulnerable curve of her mouth down to the thrust of her breasts under the thick sweater. Reminding her silently that layers of clothing were no protection at all.

He said, 'But you chose not to accompany them.'

She looked away. 'It was never really an option. I—I needed to find permanent work. And, of course, I still do.'

'So this time at Terauze is your own—interlude, *peut-être*?'

'No,' she said. 'More like being caught between a rock and a hard place. But I came here to work, so if you'll explain the routine, I can get started.'

'There is no hurry,' he said with a shrug. 'First become accustomed to a new country and a new life.'

'But I want to do my share,' she said vehemently. 'I've no intention of being just a—a kept woman, however temporary. I need to know you're getting your money's worth.'

His face suddenly relaxed into a wicked grin. '*Vraiment?*' he drawled.

'Then it is only necessary to have my clothes brought here to this room, and everything arranges itself.'

'Like hell it does.' It was difficult to sound positive when she was blushing again, her body burning up. 'I haven't the slightest intention of sleeping with you.'

'Believe me, *ma belle,* sleeping was not my purpose either.' Andre was laughing openly now. 'But, if you insist, I can wait until you are my wife.'

'Something else that is never going to happen,' she said defiantly.

'*Alors,* if you wish a task to perform,' Andre went on as if she hadn't spoken, 'then you can come down and make me some coffee and we can drink it while we talk.'

She said quickly, 'I don't want any coffee—and I need to tidy my room.'

The firm mouth twisted. 'Even though we both know that there are things to be said? Questions still to be answered?'

She forced a smile. 'Even so. I—I don't want to make more work for Madame Rameau.'

There was a silence, then he said quietly, 'As you wish. Then we shall meet again at lunch, *a midi et demi.*'

As soon as he'd gone, Ginny got out her mobile phone and keyed in the Welburns' number. To her surprise, the call was taken not by the housekeeper but Jonathan, who seemed equally astonished to be hearing from her.

'Where on earth are you?' he demanded.

'In France,' she said over-brightly. 'Visiting Andrew's other family.' Which, she hoped would confer a kind of respectability on the trip. She paused. 'But there's rather a snag. I need to speak to Mother and Cilla fairly urgently and I can't remember the name of their hotel. Can you remind me?'

'Your solicitor has already asked me, and I have no idea.' There was a chill in his voice. 'Your sister left me a message as brief as it was uninformative. And Mrs Pelham says that neither Cilla nor your mother took their phones. So we're all in the dark.'

Ginny said uncomfortably, 'I think it was all last minute and very rushed.'

He said bluntly, 'I'm afraid I don't find that much of a consolation. Not when Cilla and I are due to be married in a few months. But it seems on a par with everything else that's been going on. Now you must excuse me. I'm on my way out.'

Ginny sank down on the edge of the bed, staring at her phone as if it might grow teeth and bite her. Because this was certainly not the response she'd expected.

What on earth had possessed her sister to put herself out of touch and out of reach on the other side of the world? And from her fiancé of all people?

Everything else that's been going on...

The words had an ominous ring about them, she thought, recalling Jon's open discontent at the dinner party.

Of course Andre had never actually admitted having an intimate liaison with Cilla. But nor had he denied that their mutual and very public attraction over dinner had continued in private, she thought, sinking her teeth into her lower lip.

But how could Cilla—when she loved Jonathan?

Maybe she couldn't help herself, said a small annoying voice in her head. Just like you.

She sighed and put her phone back in her bag. If there were to be many more calls to England, she would need to top it up with money as well as recharge the battery.

But maybe that wouldn't be necessary if, as she hoped and prayed, she would soon be on her way back to a new life and a worthwhile career. If Andre kept his part of their bargain.

And as long as she didn't have to keep hers…

She looked down at herself. Pressed a hand against the flatness of her abdomen, telling herself that everything would be all right and she had nothing to worry about. That Fate wouldn't play her such a dirty trick.

Telling herself, too, that she needed to stop brooding and find something else to occupy her mind.

She'd offered an obvious fib about her room, which was already immaculate, so she retrieved the thriller she'd bought at the airport, stretched out on the bed and began to read, keeping an eye on her little clock as she did so.

When she presented herself punctually in the kitchen, she found the meal more than lived up to its promise, the chicken falling off the bone and the vegetables perfectly cooked in the rich and subtly flavoured sauce.

To her own astonishment, Ginny ate every scrap of the generous portion she was given and still found room for a large slice of *tarte tatin* under Madame Rameau's indulgent gaze.

In faulty but robust English, she informed Ginny that she was too thin. That a breeze of the most small would carry her away, *enfin,* and a man liked a woman that he knew he was holding in his arms.

And no prizes for guessing what man she was referring to, thought Ginny, avoiding Andre's sardonic glance across the table, and furious to find herself blushing again, as if she was going for some all-time record in embarrassment.

When the meal was over, Andre said, 'I have to go back to Dijon this afternoon, Virginie, so there is no need for you to hide away in your room again. Clothilde, who believes you need rest, has lit the fire for you in *le petit salon,* which you will find more comfortable.' He paused. 'Also some of my mother's books are there. Please choose anything you want.'

'Thank you,' she returned stiffly.

'That is, of course, unless you wish to come with me. You might enjoy seeing Dijon in daylight.' He added softly, 'And it could appeal in other ways.'

'That's kind of you.' She tried to ignore the swift unwelcome shiver of her senses at the thought of what they might be. 'However, I'd prefer to wait until I take the flight home.'

'As you wish.' His shrug was unperturbed. 'Although you may wait a long time. But the choice is naturally yours.'

As if I'm here of my own free will, Ginny thought rebelliously as she returned his '*Au revoir.*'

Once he'd departed, Madame Rameau decisively rejected any help with clearing away, and conducted Ginny through another door into what she realised was the main entrance hall.

Baronial, Ginny thought as she looked around her, doesn't get near it. There was an enormous fireplace, easily able to accommodate an average ox at the far end, while the centre was occupied by the biggest table she'd ever seen, its length measured by a series of elaborate silver candelabra. If that was where dinner would be held, any conversation would need to be shouted.

Nor was the *petit salon* particularly small. And although the furnishings were definitely more shabby than chic, the room looked inviting, with the pale sun coming through the long windows and logs crackling in the grate.

In the centre of the marble mantelpiece was a charming ormolu clock, clearly dating from a different century, flanked by two exquisitely pretty porcelain candlesticks, and a photograph in a silver frame.

A family group, she realised, with a slender dark-haired, brown-eyed woman at the centre, her tranquil features lit by a glowing smile, her hand resting on the shoulder of an adolescent boy, while a broad-shouldered man stood protectively behind them.

Even at half his age, Andre was unmistakable, she thought. And now that she'd had her first look at his mother, she could see what Mrs Pel had meant. No beauty, certainly, but with a sweetness about her that shone through.

While Bertrand Duchard, whom she would meet that evening, had a tough, uncompromising face which seemed to warn 'Don't mess with me'.

And I was hoping for twinkly-eyed benevolence, she mocked herself as she turned away, deciding that before she left Terauze for ever, she would offer Andre the photo of his father she'd brought with her to fill the space on the other side of the clock.

This, after all, was where Andrew had really wanted to be, in exchange for his beautiful, luxurious home and his standing in the community. His marriage...

He might never have persuaded Rosina to get this far, she mused wryly. But she'd been his wife, for better, for worse, and surely she'd deserved, at least, to be given the option.

Yet, for some unfathomable reason, she thought restively, he believed I'd fit right in. In heaven's name why?

She'd intended to continue with her thriller but it was upstairs, so she wandered over to the tall glass-fronted bookcase to see if she could find something more engaging. She discovered a mixture from Dickens, Hardy and Tolkien to modern detective stories mingling with some interesting literary fiction.

In addition she found Flaubert's *Madame Bovary* and several novels by Honoré de Balzac and Dumas both in the original and in English translations, plus a well-thumbed French grammar, suggesting that the late Madame Duchard had been working to improve her knowledge of her adopted language.

A worthy ambition which I've no wish to emulate, she told herself with determination. It smacks too much of making myself at home—which I'm not and never will be.

In the end, out of sheer nostalgia, she picked *The Hobbit* and retired with it to the elderly but still comfortable sofa facing the fire.

But perhaps she knew the story too well because, after a while, she found her mind drifting.

The result, she thought, pulling a cushion under her cheek, of the warmth of the room and the large lunch which had preceded it. Whatever, it would do no harm to close her eyes for a minute.

When she opened them again with a start, the room was in darkness and the logs in the fireplace had burned away to ashes.

My God, she thought, struggling upright and pushing her hair back from her face. I must have slept for hours.

And she'd dreamed. Dreamed she was back at Barrowdean, walking through a series of empty unfamiliar rooms, searching desperately for— something. Eventually hearing in the echoing distance the deep-throated bark of a dog, and calling 'Barney' begun to run.

I must have said it aloud, she told herself, and that's what woke me.

Only there it was again, the sound of a bark, gruff, excited and close at hand. She turned to stare towards the door. It opened and light flooded the room at the press of a switch. Then, with a scrabble of paws, Barney was there hurling himself across the room at her, paws up against her chest and licking every inch he could reach. No dream, but solid golden reality.

'Barney. Oh, darling boy.' She was off the sofa, kneeling on the rug with her arms round him, her face wet with sudden uncontrollable tears.

She looked over his head at Andre lounging in the doorway, his face inscrutable. 'Oh—how did you find him?'

'He was never lost.' He paused. 'Or did you believe I would leave him in England?'

'But surely there are rules and regulations about taking dogs abroad. Vaccinations—paperwork—stuff like that.'

'Already completed by my father. I had only to change the dates of Barney's collection and flight.'

'He flew?'

'*Bien sûr.* There are companies that specialise in such arrangements.'

'I didn't know.' She bent and put her cheek against the golden head. 'I—I thought I'd never see him again. You could have told me.'

He shrugged. 'Or you could have asked. *Alors,* it was Marguerite who told me of your distress at your mother's ultimatum. Not you.'

She flushed. 'My mother has never liked dogs. And I didn't think you'd care.'

'You have much to learn,' he said flatly. His gaze

travelled from the sofa to the dead fire. 'You have been asleep?'

'Well, yes.' She got to her feet. 'Perhaps Madame was right and I did need a rest after all.'

There was an odd silence, then he said quietly, 'She is rarely wrong.' He clicked his fingers and Barney went to him, tail like a metronome, pushing his head against the long jeans-clad legs just as he'd always done with Andrew, forcing Ginny to bite her lip hard.

She said, 'I don't know how to thank you for this.'

He said softly, *Vraiment*? Yet I can think of many ways, each more pleasurable than the last.'

Her flush deepened. She said unevenly, 'You don't make being here any easier for me with remarks like that.'

'And when you are my wife,' he said, 'will you expect me still to guard my tongue, or shall I be allowed to tell you that I want you and how I intend to please you in bed?'

There was a note in his voice that made her breath catch in her throat and sent an unwelcome trembling sensation rippling across her nerve endings.

Hastily, she pulled herself together. 'You may be

certain this marriage will happen,' she said curtly, 'but I'm not.'

'*C'est ce que nous verrons,*' he said, and smiled at her. 'That, *ma mie,* remains to be seen.' He turned and went out, Barney padding beside him.

She followed them both to the kitchen. Barney's feeding bowl and water dish were in the scullery area, but his basket was by the hearth and he went straight to it and sat looking round him.

She said, 'He's had quite a traumatic time. A plane trip and now finding himself in strange surroundings.'

'But not with strangers.' Andre bent to fondle Barney's ears—a gesture she remembered. 'And the girl who accompanied him said he was a born traveller.'

'All the same,' Ginny went on quickly, 'I think I'd better stay quietly here this evening. Help him settle down.'

He said blandly, 'There is no need for that, *ma mie.* He too is one of the family now and will dine with us.'

Damn, thought Ginny, who hadn't seen that coming. I can't say I'm tired, having slept most of the afternoon, and if I complain of a headache, he'll probably have a whole cupboard full of painkillers.

So it looks as if I'll just have to make the best of this dinner *en famille*, even though I'd rather be a hundred miles away and still travelling. Not stopping until I reach some place where life will be simple again.

And knew with a pang that achieving her ambition would not be as easy as it sounded.

Ginny rarely bothered with cosmetics but, she told herself, on this occasion she needed all the help she could get, especially as the most respectable garment she possessed was the grey skirt she'd worn for Andrew's funeral, teamed this time with a paler grey scoop-necked sweater.

Not exactly gala gear, but better than the taupe dress, she thought ruefully, as she applied a touch of blusher to her face and emphasised her eyes with silvery shadow and a soft grey pencil. Her only lipstick was a neutral shade between pink and beige, but it would have to do.

After a swift spray of scent, she gave herself a last, critical glance in the mirror and went downstairs.

Jules was sitting at the kitchen table and he looked across at her with open surprise, then across at Andre, his lips forming into a silent whistle. Andre merely grinned back at him.

One of those male bonding moments that women love so much, thought Ginny, biting her lip and wondering if her neckline wasn't a little too scooped.

'Papa is waiting for us in the *grand salon*,' Andre informed her. 'Tonight the Château Terauze is *en fête* in your honour, *ma belle.*'

He snapped his fingers and Barney uncurled himself from his basket and came to join them, padding sedately between them as they crossed the great hall.

Suddenly nervous, Ginny cast about for something to say and came up with, 'Does Jules have a girlfriend?'

'A new one every week,' he responded. 'Why do you ask? Are you thinking of adding to their number?'

She wondered how he'd react if she said, Actually, I fancy him rotten, but decided not to take the risk.

Instead, she said caustically, 'Out of the frying pan into the fire? Hardly. I was just—curious.'

'You are not the only one. According to Clothilde,

his mother despairs that she will not live to see her grandchildren.'

'Is she very ill?'

'Only in her imagination,' he returned laconically and she was startled into a giggle.

He smiled too, then reached down and took her hand. His clasp was light, but she felt it in every curve and every hollow of her body, as if they were, once again, naked, their bodies locked together in the ultimate intimacy. In the act of madness which had brought her here, she thought restraining a gasp, along with the impulse to wrench herself free.

Then he pushed open a door and, as they entered the brilliantly lit room beyond, Ginny realised that this time a gasp might not have been out of place.

Imposingly furnished with pastel silk wallpaper and formally grouped chairs and small sofas, all striped satin and narrow gilded legs, this room was as far removed from *le petit salon* as it was possible to get.

In fact, thought Ginny, it was more like a showcase of a bygone era than a sitting room.

Even the fire seemed elegant, burning modestly in its elaborate marble fireplace.

And beside it, languidly occupying one of the

small armchairs, shapely legs crossed and looking as if Chanel had invented the little black dress
solely for her, was Monique Chaloux.

For a moment, Ginny felt Andre's fingers tighten
round hers, then he released her as the man standing on the other side of the fireplace came forward,
smiling. He was of medium height and trimly built
with broad shoulders, his rugged features set off
by a mane of silver hair, but still recognisable from
the photograph.

'Andre, *mon gars,*' he said with open affection
and embraced him.

As Andre returned his stepfather's greeting with
equal warmth, Barney wandered forward to explore these new surroundings.

'*Mon Dieu.*' Languor forgotten, Mademoiselle
Chaloux was on her feet. 'A clumsy, dirty animal in the Baronne Laure's beautiful *salon*?' She
looked at Ginny. 'Is the dog yours, *mademoiselle*?'

Andre said quietly, 'He belonged to my father,
Monique, therefore he is mine. And he has perfect manners.'

A commendation instantly spoiled by Barney's
low, menacing growl aimed straight at his detrac-
tor.

Mademoiselle Chaloux recoiled. 'And dangerous too,' she accused shrilly. 'Bertrand—I insist the animal must wear a muzzle.'

'Please, no.' Ginny intervened hastily. 'He's never growled at anyone before.' Not even Rosina at her worst, she thought. 'Truly. He—he's had a trying day.'

The other woman snorted. *'Quelle bêtise.'*

Bertrand Duchard extended a hand for Barney to sniff. 'I would not call him a danger,' he said calmly. 'More—a new friend who needs a little time.'

He turned to Ginny. 'And now, *mademoiselle,* permit me to welcome you. *Je suis énchante de faire votre connaissance.'*

Not that enchanted, thought Ginny, aware that his smile no longer reached his eyes.

She said quietly, 'You're very kind, Monsieur le Baron. Your home is very beautiful.'

'You have heard about it, perhaps, from your *beau-père?*

'No,' she said. 'He—he never mentioned it.'

There was a silence, then the Baron inclined his head courteously. 'Then it is good we meet at last, as he wished. Andre, you must make sure your guest's stay with us is a pleasant one. Burgundy, *mademoiselle,* has a fascinating history and some exquisite architecture.'

He turned to Mademoiselle Chaloux. 'Ring the bell, will you, Monique, and Gaston will bring the *aperitifs* to toast our visitor.'

It all sounded very hospitable and pleasant but Ginny wasn't fooled.

'He doesn't want me here,' she whispered to herself. 'I'm getting a subtle warning not to outstay my welcome.'

Maybe she had an ally at last, yet somehow she couldn't rejoice, because suddenly it was being brought home to her, coldly and bleakly, that she no longer belonged anywhere.

And the lonely, painful knowledge of that settled inside her like a stone.

CHAPTER NINE

THE ENSUING SILENCE was eventually broken by the Baron's courteous voice. 'Your mother is well, *mademoiselle,* and your sister?'

'Thank you, yes. They've gone away for a little while.'

'And you did not choose to accompany them?' asked Monique Chaloux.

Ginny knew an overwhelming temptation to say affably, No, because I'm flat broke and the future Baron thinks he may have made me pregnant. But she restrained herself nobly with a quiet, 'No, not this time.'

Then the door opened and a small thin man, his solemn face made even more lugubrious by a heavy dark moustache, came in carrying a tray of glasses filled with something pink and sparkling.

The Baron said, '*Merci,* Gaston. You have tried Kir Royale, *mademoiselle?*'

She took a glass. 'Yes, and loved it. *Crème de cassis* and champagne. Wonderful.'

'Ah, but it is not champagne,' Andre said swiftly. 'Our *cremant du Bourgogne* is made by a similar method, but the name "champagne" can only be used for wine that comes from its own region around Epernay. The rules are strict.'

Ginny frowned. 'I didn't realise it could be so complex.'

'We take great pride in our industry, and in what each region has to offer. And the *crème de cassis* is also made in Burgundy.' Andre raised his glass. '*À votre santé.*'

She wondered if his choice of toast was loaded, her state of health being an issue between them, but echoed it anyway and sipped, before taking the chair she was offered and discovering it was just as uncomfortable as it looked. Perhaps, she mused, the enormous skirts and masses of petticoats favoured by ladies in the olden days acted as a bolster.

She took another look round her. There were numerous pictures on the walls, mostly landscapes in frames as gilded as the furniture. The exception was the portrait of a woman, which hung above the fireplace.

A stern, rather cold beauty, her black hair drawn back from her face into a chignon, and the *décolleté* of her dark red dress revealing an elaborate necklace of what seemed to be rubies.

'You are admiring the Baronne Laure, Monsieur Bertrand's mother, I see.' Monique Chaloux leaned forward. 'An excellent likeness. It is a Terauze tradition that a portrait of the Baronne always hangs in this room and, in her case, most appropriate as she redesigned it so admirably.' She sighed. 'Sadly, it seems, *notre chère* Linnet would never consent to be painted.'

'My wife,' Bertrand Duchard said quietly, 'was a very modest woman.'

'But of course,' Mademoiselle agreed quickly, smiling, but Ginny read quite clearly in that smile *and with so much to be modest about* and it galled her.

She said impulsively, 'Surely it isn't too late. There's a lovely photograph of her in the other sitting room. Couldn't someone paint a portrait from that?'

Andre said slowly, '*Et pourquoi pas?*' He looked at the Baron. 'What do you think, Papa?'

'That it would be a joy to see my dear one remembered in such a way.'

He looked at Ginny with undisguised surprise. '*Merci, mademoiselle.* An excellent thought.'

Which was an improvement. However, Madame's softly spoken, 'Bravo, indeed,' left Ginny with the uncomfortable feeling she had just made an enemy.

She was quite glad when Gaston came to summon them to dinner, in a much cosier room hung with tapestries of medieval hunting scenes, in which, she noticed, the central figure was a tall man with a long, slightly hooked nose and clothing that glimmered with gold.

'Philippe Le Hardi. Duke Philip the Bold,' Andre supplied quietly. 'An amazing man, at one time King of France in all but name, and the creator of the Order of the Golden Fleece. His feasts were legendary and so was his spending. He died poor.'

'But we remember him,' said Bertrand, 'for his interest in the wine industry and the measures he took to protect its quality, which led, in time, to the Appellation Contrôlée system.'

Monique Chaloux flung up her hands. 'Have pity, *messieurs*. You forget that Mademoiselle Mason is not Dominique Lavaux and this talk of wine will bore her. Let us speak instead of your plans for her entertainment while she is with us.' She paused. 'You will make time for a little sightseeing, *n'est-ce pas*?'

There was a brief odd silence, and Ginny saw Andre's mouth tighten. He said calmly, 'As soon as the pruning is finished, and begin, I think, with Beaune. Would that please you, Virginie?'

'Thank you,' she returned swiftly. 'But it's really not necessary. You have work to do, and I have plenty to read, and Barney to take for walks. I'll be fine.'

Monique Chaloux clapped her hands. 'The perfect guest.'

But not Dominique Lavaux, thought Ginny. And wondered.

The meal, served by Gaston, began with *consommé,* moved on to some excellent smoked fish patties with a creamy sauce, followed by grilled steak, served with a *gratin dauphinois* and green beans.

'Charolais beef,' said Bertrand with satisfaction. 'The best in the world.'

Ginny, helping herself to Dijon mustard, decided it would be impolitic to speak up for Aberdeen Angus. Too many undercurrents already, she thought.

Dinner concluded with *crème brûlée* and a selection of local cheeses. Ginny sat back in her chair with a little sigh. 'That was a wonderful meal.'

'No better than the one you served to me,' Andre said lightly and smiled at her across the table.

And for once, she realised, there was no edge or mockery to his smile, just a warmth that seemed to reach out and touch her, spreading its tendrils over every inch of her body. Holding her transfixed and making it suddenly difficult to think or to breathe...

And heard some inner voice whisper with longing, *Andre*...

'Do not let Gaston hear you, Andre.' Monique's brisk voice broke the spell. 'Or he may tell his wife and she will make our stomachs suffer for it.' She paused. 'Shall we take coffee in the *salon*?'

'We will join you later, if you please,' said Bertrand, adding blandly, 'I need to speak with my son on the boring topic of wine.'

The coffee, though strong and delicious, was served in tiny, fragile cups balancing awkwardly on their saucers, while Ginny, in turn, balanced on the edge of a spindly chair.

One false move, she thought wryly, and Baronne Laure's satin upholstery will never be the same again.

For a while there was silence, except for the

crackling of the logs in the grate and Barney's faint snores from the exquisite pastel rug, then Mademoiselle leaned forward. 'Tell me, *mademoiselle,* how long do you intend to stay at Terauze?'

'I'm not really sure,' she returned with guarded truth.

'Then am I permitted to offer some advice?'

Apart from putting a hand over the woman's mouth and wrestling her to the floor, Ginny could see no way of preventing it, so she murmured something non-committal and waited warily.

'If you have any romantic dreams about Monsieur Andre, abandon them now.' Mademoiselle's voice was low, almost intense. 'He can be charming, and women find him attractive.' Her mouth twisted into a faint sneer. 'Something of which he takes full advantage, believe me, although his preference is for beautiful blondes. But never seriously or for very long, as his lovers soon discover.' She shrugged. 'Perhaps, in this, he resembles his true father.'

Ginny swallowed back the hot denial rising to her lips, saying evenly, 'Mr Charlton was a good man. I think he genuinely loved Andre's mother. Besides which, one affair hardly makes him a serial seducer.' She paused, her throat tightening painfully. 'As for Andre, his private life is not my concern. Or perhaps I don't take him seriously either.'

'*Vous avez raison.* Marriage is a serious business, and Andre is not the material from which good husbands are made.' She examined her immaculate nails. 'His wife, you understand, will need to be a girl of discretion, someone from his own world who can also contribute to the *domaine.*'

Ginny said quietly, 'Then it's fortunate that I have no interest in being married.' Which, she told herself defensively, was no more than the truth.

Mademoiselle's brows lifted. 'Then why, with Monsieur Charlton gone, did you accept such an invitation?'

The million-dollar question.

Ginny said carefully, 'Perhaps I too needed to get away from the trauma of the last few weeks. And I admit I was curious about this part of my stepfather's life, *mademoiselle.*'

'And when your curiosity is satisfied?'

'I intend to go back to England.' And offered a silent prayer that there'd be nothing to prevent her. Or, at least, that she could convince Andre it was so.

Monique Chaloux's nod suggested she too was satisfied. 'You are wise. Whatever your *beau-père* may have hoped, *mademoiselle,* there is nothing for you here, except heartbreak perhaps.' She paused. 'Permit me to offer you more coffee.'

Ginny managed a polite refusal. She had just eaten a delicious meal, but she felt as hollow inside as if she'd fasted for a week. Shaken too.

Which was ridiculous, because how could the revelation that Andre was an experienced and predatory womaniser really come as any kind of surprise after the way he'd behaved with her?

I must have been one of his easiest conquests, she told herself bitterly as self-disgust attacked her again.

And presumably this Dominique Lavaux has all the necessary attributes of a future Baronne, even if I am temporarily occupying her bed.

Barney stirred, lifting his head, then got up, tail wagging, padding towards the door as it opened and the men came in, laughing together, and even with just a sideways glance across the room, Ginny felt her entire body clench in a sudden shock of need, and knew it was no wonder if women collapsed like ninepins under the sheer force of Andre's attraction.

What she must not do was let it happen to her. Not again.

Now she watched Barney gently head-butt Andre's long legs in welcome, as if underlining his change of allegiance. And felt as if she'd never been so much alone in her life.

After that, the party broke up fairly soon, Mademoiselle Chaloux insisting prettily that she had an early start in the morning. 'They say the weather will become warmer tomorrow,' she added with a mock shiver. 'Like my mother, I find the winters harsh here compared with Provence.'

The Baron also excused himself on the grounds of having paperwork to attend to, and, to Ginny's relief, Andre showed no wish to linger among the stripes and gilding.

'You are very quiet,' he observed as they entered the kitchen, neat, empty and silent apart from the hum of the dishwasher. 'Did Monique bore you with more praise of Baronne Laure and her exquisite taste?'

She didn't bore me at all, thought Ginny, with a pang. She forced a smile. 'No, but perhaps she guessed it was a lost cause. The furniture may be valuable, but I prefer comfort.'

'It was certainly expensive,' he returned drily.

'Papa says that one of the few times my grandfather lost his temper with her was when he discovered she'd been fooled by someone she'd met at a party into paying Louis Quinze prices for reproduction junk.

'*Heureusement,* it ended her dalliance with interior décor.' He smiled at her. 'But if you have any ideas for improvements to the château, I would be delighted to hear them.'

Ginny bit her lip. He was talking about a situation that could not—must not exist, she thought resentfully. Acting as if they were an actual couple in love and planning their future home. Something she could not allow to go on, but was not sure how to stop.

She said, 'I was surprised to see Mademoiselle Chaloux tonight.'

Andre shrugged. 'But I was not,' he replied tersely. 'Monique has her own agenda to pursue.'

'She's a close friend?'

'But an employee. A few days a week, she maintains the records for the house and the *domaine* and keeps the accounts, all with great efficiency.' He paused. 'Also, she hopes to marry Papa Bertrand.'

'Oh, I see.' Ginny swallowed. 'Do you think she will?'

'I try, *ma belle,* not to think about it at all,' he drawled. 'But I trust most sincerely that she will be disappointed.'

She said slowly, 'She mentioned Provence. Wasn't that where your mother's friend went to live?'

'*Mais oui.* Monique was the friend on whom Maman so mistakenly relied. She stayed in Provence until a few weeks after my mother's funeral, then returned alone.' He added drily, 'Presumably she had another *correspondante* who kept her informed.'

Ginny gasped. 'You mean she—waited to come back until your mother was dead?'

'There would have been little point in returning while Maman lived.'

He paused. 'Clothilde has always claimed that Monique, as a girl, threw herself at Papa constantly, and left Terauze with her parents only when she realised that his heart was already given to her little English friend.'

His mouth curled contemptuously. 'One should not accept too readily Mademoiselle's references to *notre chère* Linnet.'

'I don't.' She paused. 'But there was something else I wanted to ask.

'Did I misunderstand, or is Gaston really married to Madame Rameau?'

There was a note almost of awe in her voice and Andre's face relaxed into a wicked grin.

'*C'est incroyable, n'est ce pas, mais c'est vrai.* And they have three big sons, married with families, two in Dijon and one in Lyon.'

'Heavens,' Ginny said weakly.

He clicked his tongue reprovingly. 'You, *ma belle,* are thinking naughty thoughts.' He discarded his jacket, hanging it on the back of a chair, then walked over to the stove. '*Du café?*'

'No, thank you,' she said quickly, deciding it was best to leave and take her naughty thoughts with her. She put a hand over her mouth as if stifling a yawn. 'I'm going to bed.'

'It is still early,' he said. 'And still I wish to talk to you. I will join you in the *petit salon,* and we will have a *digestif* together.'

As she hesitated, he added softly, '*S'il te plaît,* Virginie,' and she found herself making her way reluctantly out of the kitchen and across the hall.

The fire in the *salon* had been rekindled at some point, and the room felt deliciously cosy. Ginny fed it with more logs before seating herself stiffly in the corner of the sofa.

When he came in, he was carrying a bottle of brandy and two glasses into which he poured generous measures before seating himself beside her.

'*A la tienne,*' he said, lifting his own glass in a toast. '*Eh bien,* what else did Monique say to make you so thoughtful?'

Ginny stared straight ahead at the leaping flames. 'Something I already knew,' she returned, choosing her words with care. 'That I don't belong here and should go home.'

There was a taut silence, then he said quietly, 'How obliging of her to interest herself in your welfare on so short an acquaintance.'

'Perhaps she was also speaking for Monsieur Bertrand,' she said quickly. 'He clearly doesn't welcome my presence.'

Andre shrugged. 'He found it a surprise, *peut-être.*'

Ginny swallowed some brandy, enjoying against her will the smooth mellow flavour. 'All the same, I want to bring this supposed visit to an end.'

'Not,' he said, 'until the situation between us has been resolved. As you agreed.'

'That was before I knew how impossible it would be. Whatever you may think, I don't like deceiving people, and I can't treat it as lightly as you seem to.'

'You are mistaken,' he said quietly. 'I regard it as seriously as you could wish.'

'In that case,' she said, 'please let me go home.'

'Home?' The query was almost contemptuous. 'To what? No vague replies. Where and how will you live?'

His words struck an unhappy chord with her own fears, pushing her into dangerous waters.

'You mean now that Andrew, my meal ticket, won't be there?' she challenged.

The dark eyes narrowed. 'Is that how you saw him?'

Think what you like...

The words hovered, but remained unspoken. She would not—could not betray Andrew's memory.

She bent her head. 'No, of course not.' She drew a shivering breath. 'I—I loved him, and I thought he cared for me.' She added wildly, 'For all of us.'

Her voice cracked suddenly as a wave of the sorrow circumstances had so far forced her to suppress finally broke over her. Overwhelmed her.

She found herself blinded, drowning in scalding tears, her throat aching and her body torn by the hot and heavy sobs she was unable to control as she mourned for Andrew.

She was dimly aware of Andre taking the glass from her hand. Felt herself enfolded, lifted across his body, her face pressed into the strong angle between his neck and shoulder and his lips against her hair as he held her.

She was aware of the crisp collar of his shirt against her cheek. The warmth of him, coupled with the evocative scent of his skin. The infinite comfort of his hand moving slowly and gently against her spine.

He said softly, 'You must not cry any more. My father was a man with disappointments in his life, but please believe that you were not one of them.'

But her tears were not so easily dammed, and she clung to him, pushing into him in a kind of desperation, as if she needed to be absorbed, utterly consumed. A mute offering of her entire self.

She heard him murmur something roughly. Then his hand was under her chin, tilting up her soaked, ruined face, and his lips found hers, parting them for the heated, irresistible invasion of his tongue.

The kiss was endless. Driven. Her hands moved on him, tracing the familiarity of bone and muscle through the linen fabric of his shirt, and stroking the strong column of his neck before twining in his dark hair.

As the demand of his mouth deepened, he pushed her top down from her shoulder together with the strap of her bra, his fingers seeking one rose-tipped breast, freeing it from its lacy cup and caressing it with delicate sensuality.

She was lost, the raw emotion of grief exploding into another very different sensation, her body arching in its own demand that was also a surrender, as she remembered the searing, exquisite pleasure of being naked in his arms. And as the desire to have him once again sheathed inside her exerted its own almost brutal pressure, impossible to be ignored or denied.

He said her name quietly and huskily. Then his mouth closed on her uncovered nipple, laving it with the tip of his tongue, before suckling it gently and voluptuously to an aching glory of need, as his hand moved downwards to push away the folds of her skirt and stroke the silken warmth of her parted thighs.

But it was not enough. She wanted to feel the arousal of his touch on her bare flesh—to relive the wonder of that first devastating awakening, and arched towards him, silently inviting him to free her from the confines of tights and briefs.

She heard him sigh softly, felt the arm that held her tighten its clasp to the brink of pain. Then he moved, lowering her slowly and with infinite care to the softness of the fur rug in front of the fireplace and following her down.

The only sound in the room was the hiss of the smouldering logs a few feet away and their own urgent breathing as they undressed each other between kisses, clumsy in their haste.

Their clothing gone, Andre's mouth left hers and began to trace a slow, lingering path down her body, exploring with minute and exquisite detail every slender curve and plane, making her shiver with delight and an anticipation she hardly understood and almost feared.

Only to feel him pause, his head lifting as he stared towards the door.

And the next second she heard it too—the faint sound of footsteps crossing the hall combined with a man's tuneless whistling and, at the same moment, in the distance, Barney's vociferous barking.

Andre said on a groan, 'Ah, *Dieu.*' He sat up, reaching for his clothes and dragging them on, then got to his feet, pushing his shirt back into his pants and raking his dishevelled hair with his fingers.

He looked down at her, his mouth twisting rue-fully.

'Gaston,' he said. 'Doing his rounds before he locks up. I had—forgotten. I will delay him in the kitchen while you cover yourself.'

When he had gone, she lay still for a moment, her dazed brain coming to terms with what had happened.

And what might have happened if Gaston had started with the *salon*, finding them naked and en-thralled in the welter of their discarded clothing.

She gave a little inarticulate cry and sat up, pull-ing on her skirt and top with frantic shaking hands and thrusting her feet back into her shoes, listen-ing to the distant murmur of voices and dread-ing their approach. Knowing that even if she was now marginally decent, she could not risk being caught there.

Her underclothing scrunched into a tight ball in her hand, she tiptoed from the *salon,* making for the main staircase, and the sanctuary of her bed-room.

Although what kind of a sanctuary was it when her door was unlocked and Andre had the key?

She sank down on the edge of the bed and covered her face with her hands.

What had happened to her? she asked herself in despair. In a matter of days, how had she gone from a relatively blameless existence to one which had her stumbling from one disaster to the next? And all of it entirely her own fault—especially tonight.

Because only Gaston's pursuance of some nightly routine had saved her from yet more abject folly, and that was the bitter truth she had to face.

Only now it must stop.

After a moment's hesitation, she fetched the chair from the dressing table, and wedged it securely under the door handle.

At least she hoped it was secure. It was something she'd read about in an old-fashioned thriller, which was no guarantee it would be proof against a strong and determined man.

Or, for that matter, a weak and stupid female...

She took off her shoes, turned off the light and got under the covers, still in her skirt and top. Listening—waiting in the darkness.

And eventually she heard it—the soft knock on the door and his voice saying her name.

She realised that he was waiting for her to invite him in—to enter her room, her bed, her body.

To complete what that strange storm of emotion had brought in its wake.

She lifted her hands, clamping them fiercely over her mouth so that no sound could escape. Not a word, a sigh or even an indrawn breath. So that he would think she was asleep, instead of lying there trying to conquer the burning, trembling ache of her unfulfilled flesh.

Knowing that her memories of his lovemaking were already a torment, hardly to be endured, and for the sake of her sanity she could risk no more.

Waiting until the heavy silence told her at last that he had gone.

CHAPTER TEN

I HAD TOO much to drink last night.

Ginny rehearsed the words in her head over and over again as she prepared reluctantly to go down to breakfast the following morning.

That was the story she was going to use, treating the whole thing lightly as an error of judgement, embarrassing but not fatal, and she would stick to it like glue, no matter how Andre might respond.

After all, it was more or less the truth, she told herself defensively, the brandy proving the final straw after the wine so generously poured at dinner. Also she seemed to have done him an injustice. The chair, now restored to its rightful place, had been an unnecessary precaution because he would never have entered the room without her consent.

Sighing, she opened the shutters and found that Mademoiselle Chaloux had been right about the weather. The sky was uniformly grey and the view of the vines was concealed by a thick drizzle. Her accuracy in other matters remained to be discovered.

At the kitchen door, she braced herself, before turning the handle and walking in.

But the room's only occupant was Madame Rameau setting a platter of bread and croissants and a jar of preserves on the table. Even Barney's basket was empty, presumably because Andre had taken him for a walk.

'*Bonjour, mademoiselle.*' Madame's shrewd eyes swept her from head to foot. '*Vous avez bien dormi?*'

'*Oui, merci,*' said Ginny, aware that she was lying. That it had been hours before she fell into a restless doze interspersed with dreams that she would much prefer to forget. She took the coffee that Madame handed to her and sat down.

All she needed to do, she thought, spreading a slice of bread with blackcurrant jam, was ask casually for Andre. Simple enough surely, when he was her host, so why did it seem so impossible? As if she was somehow exhibiting their entire relationship for inspection?

'You look pale, little one, and not happy.' Madame sounded almost severe. 'And you will be *plus contente, peut-être,* when you know more of

Terauze and the life here. So, later, when the rain has stopped, you will take a little *promenade* with me to the village, *n'est-ce pas*?'

She nodded briskly. 'And do not disturb yourself, *mon enfant,* if you are stared at. Everything that occurs here is of interest to the whole of Terauze, and it's natural that your arrival should cause a *brouhaha.* But all will be well. Clothilde gives you her word. And now I shall feed the chickens.' She bustled away, leaving Ginny to finish her *tartine.*

She was just clearing the table when the Baron came in, looking harassed and muttering under his breath in a way that told her he was swearing.

He checked when he saw Ginny. 'Your pardon, *mademoiselle.* I did not know you were here.'

'Is something wrong?'

'A problem with the computer, *hélas.*'

'Is it all right now?'

He sighed impatiently. 'No, it is beyond me. And Monique does not work today.'

'But Monsieur Andre will be back soon...'

'That will not be for some hours, *mademoiselle,*' he interrupted curtly. 'And I need urgently to access some figures.'

Giving her an opportunity to justify her presence here.

She said quietly, 'I used computers at home and at work in England, *monsieur*, so I know a little about office systems. Perhaps I could help.'

His hesitation lasted less than an instant. 'If so, I would indeed be grateful.'

He took her across the hall to a door on the other side, opening on to a flight of steep stone stairs, winding upwards.

Good God, thought Ginny as she climbed. I'm inside a tower. And what's waiting for me at the top? Monique Chaloux crouched over a spinning wheel, hoping that I'll prick my finger and sleep for a hundred years?

Instead, she found herself in a circular room that had been transformed from medieval austerity into a functional and well-equipped office with a large desk holding a computer stationed right in its centre.

She halted, entranced. 'What a wonderful place to work.'

The Baron's look held faint surprise. 'I am gratified that you think so.' He added quietly, 'It was chosen by my wife.'

'I don't blame her.' A series of windows had been set into the curve of the outer wall, and Ginny walked over and knelt on the cushioned seat be-

neath them, enjoying, in spite of the rain, a pan-
oramic view of the vineyard and the area of thick
woodland which adjoined it.

She turned away and crossed to the desk. As
she'd suspected, the system on the computer was
familiar, if totally out of date, so she had little trouble retrieving the information the Baron required,
although the pages of figures seemed confusing.

'I think you might find this easier to read on a
spreadsheet, *monsieur*,' Ginny said as she pressed
'Print'. 'And your security is very old-fashioned,
which could be dangerous. For example, I can't
see how to back up the files. Has Mademoiselle
Chaloux never mentioned these things?'

The Baron shrugged. 'She seems content to work
in her own way, *mademoiselle*. And I know little
about technology.' He paused. 'But please accept
my most sincere and grateful thanks for your assistance. And perhaps you could suggest some improvements to the system to Monique.'

Ginny said drily, 'I think she would regard that
as arrant interference, *monsieur*. After all, I'm only
a visitor here.'

He studied her for a moment, his brows lifting.
'*Peut-être, vous avez raison, mademoiselle.* Then
speak first to Andre. If the suggestions come from

him, then she must listen. He is as much her employer as I am.'

Which did not suggest he saw the lady as a future wife. Or that he looked on Ginny's own presence as anything more than temporary.

Which, of course, was a good thing, she thought as she followed him downstairs. Wasn't it?

As Madame Rameau had predicted, the rain eased off during the morning, allowing a watery sun to make its appearance, so the village tour took place as planned.

It wasn't a lengthy operation. Terauze was a cluster of narrow streets all leading on to a central square, where the daily market was just beginning to pack up, its stalls clustering round the statue of a man, standing high on a stone plinth.

Madame pointed. 'See, *mademoiselle.* That is Baron Emile who planted the first vineyard at Terauze.' She sighed. 'Each year at the Château, it was the custom to invite the village and our neighbours to celebrate his birthday, but no longer. Not after Madame Linnet was taken from us. It was as if Monsieur Bertrand could not bear such an occasion without her.'

She sighed again and walked on, but her subdued mood soon vanished as she was greeted with jovial familiarity on all sides. However, Ginny was soon aware that she was indeed the real focus of all this interest, and that whispers and stares were following her as she was marched round the square, past the *mairie* where the tricolour flew, in a kind of royal progress, which took in the bakery, the *patisserie,* the butcher's shop and the *charcuterie.*

Next was the *farmacie,* but as Madame had been accosted and engaged in animated conversation by a woman who was clearly an old friend, Ginny, seized by a sudden idea, slipped inside alone.

As she entered, two women, standing at the counter and talking to a thin-faced woman in a white coat, turned, alerted by the shop bell, and regarded her with the same curiosity she had attracted outside, but lacking the *bonhomie.*

Ginny hesitated, her immediate impulse being to back out into the street again. Because, she realised, her bright idea had just turned into Mission Impossible. Even if she'd been able to recognise the French brand names, how could she possibly buy a pregnancy testing kit when the news would be all round Terauze almost before she'd been handed her change?

And however keen she was to know the result—

to reassure herself that she would soon be free to leave—she couldn't allow that to become a subject of common gossip.

'*Vous voulez quelque chose, mademoiselle?*' The thin woman was coming forward unsmilingly.

Ginny thought quickly. 'Aspirins, *s'il vous plaît, madame,*' she hazarded, and received a sour nod in return.

She was paying for the tablets when the door opened to admit Madame Rameau in a swirl of cape. Her greeting to the woman in the white coat and her other customers was civil but brisk, and Ginny found herself shepherded firmly into the street again.

'She didn't seem very friendly,' she commented.

Madame snorted. 'Madame Donati and her husband think I am a rival for their business. *Quelle absurdité.*' She added darkly, 'Also she is a close friend, that one, of Mademoiselle Monique, who rents the *appartement* above their shop.'

'And who isn't friendly either,' Ginny said ruefully. 'Or not to me.'

Madame shrugged. 'You are English, *mademoiselle,* and another Englishwoman captured the heart of the man she wanted. That she cannot forget or forgive.'

She added, '*Moi,* I am disliked because I was there and saw it all. But it is long ago and one cannot change the past.' She saw Ginny's involuntary wince and looked at the painkillers with disfavour. '*Vous avez un mal de tête?* Better I make you a *tisane.*'

Better if I was still in England where I belong, thought Ginny wearily, as they started out of the village towards the long hill that led back to the château.

And a thousand times better if I could alter the past, so that Andre and I would never meet. And that I would not be feeling the pain that's within me now—eating me alive. Tearing me apart.

On the way, they were overtaken by a young woman on horseback, her long blonde hair tied back. Attractive, certainly, thought Ginny, but with features too strongly marked for real beauty.

She raised her riding crop in response as Madame greeted her. '*Bonjour, mademoiselle. Ça va?*' Then looked Ginny over, her eyes narrowing, before riding on.

'Who was that?'

Madame pursed her lips. 'Dominique Lavaux.' She added, 'Her uncle owns a parcel of land adjacent to our *domaine*. She is also the godchild of Mademoiselle Chaloux.'

Well, you asked, thought Ginny. And now you know.

Back at the château, she admitted mendaciously to the headache and accepted the *tisane* with its pleasant, slightly smoky flavour that Madame brewed for her before retiring to her bedroom.

She removed her coat and kicked off her boots, then lay down on the bed, on top of the covers.

Where something—whether it was the *tisane* or the walk, the fresh air or the deep solid comfort of the mattress—persuaded her taut body and troubled senses to relax, assuring her that it would do no harm to close her eyes and drift—just for a moment—in the pale afternoon light.

But when she awoke, it was to the glow of the lamps that flanked the bed, signifying that hours rather than minutes had passed. Moreover, she realised with alarm, she was no longer alone. Because Andre was sitting in an armchair a few feet away, his face brooding, even bleak as he stared down at the floor, his hands loosely clasped round his knees.

She was struck by the sudden unexpected agony of wanting above all else to go to him and take him in her arms, holding his head against her breasts as she stroked his hair and told him everything would be all right.

Which, of course, it never could be, because he looked like a man realising what an afternoon's folly in an English hotel room had actually cost him, and struggling to come to terms with his bitter regrets.

She stirred uneasily, trying to sit up, and his head lifted sharply.

He said, 'Your headache—it has gone?'

'Yes, I—I think so.' She bit her lip. 'Is that why you're here—to ask about my health?'

He said slowly, 'No, that is not the only reason.'

She thought, aware of a swift stammer in her heartbeat, Oh God, he's going to tell me that if I say again I want to leave, he won't prevent it any longer.

And why is it only now—*now*—at this moment that I know it's the last thing in the world I want to happen?

And if I leave, however will I be able to bear it?

Aware that she was holding her breath, she waited for him to speak.

He said haltingly, 'Virginie, I wish to ask your pardon for last night. I had no right to behave as

I did, having given my word, and I am ashamed. Please believe that I intended no more than to offer you some comfort.'

He paused, his eyes searching hers with a kind of desperation, and she knew that he had more to say but could not find the words.

Words that could destroy her.

She said quickly, 'I'm sorry too. I was—upset. I'd also had more than usual to drink. But I would have come to my senses before any more harm was done.'

'Harm,' he repeated. 'Is that how you regard what has happened between us since we met?'

'What else?' She gave him a defiant look. 'We made a terrible mistake, but we don't have to wreck our lives because of it.'

'Nor should we damage the future of the child you may be carrying.'

'Even if that's true, I know that to stay here and marry you would be a disaster.'

The dark brows lifted. 'How can you be so certain—and so soon?'

How indeed? she thought desperately. What argument could she possibly produce as a clincher?

'Because, when you came to England, marriage must have been the last thing on your mind.'

His mouth twisted. 'It has been mentioned. But, like most men, it has not been a priority for me so far.'

She took a deep, steadying breath. 'And because we don't—love each other.'

'Love?' Andre repeated the word musingly, as if he had never heard it before. 'When did that become part of our bargain?'

Bargain, she repeated silently. Deal—trade-off—call it what she might, how could she ever have thought it would be enough? Or, from that first moment, had she been secretly hoping for so much more?

Oh, you idiot, she thought. You pathetic little fool.

She swallowed. 'You—you're right. It didn't. I expressed myself badly, so I'll try again. I'm not your type, and you're certainly not mine.'

The dark brows lifted. 'So, what is your type? The estimable Monsieur Welburn?'

'If that's what you want to think.' She tried to sound nonchalant. 'What I really mean is—I don't want you.'

'*Vraiment?*' His tone expressed polite interest. 'And yet we both know that if Gaston had not interrupted us, we would have spent the night here in that bed and you would have woken in my arms this morning.'

She made herself shrug. 'As I said—brandy and emotion. A lethal combination, never to be repeated.'

I should forget about teaching, and become an actress, she thought painfully. I could almost convince myself.

'Something I shall try to remember while you remain with us.' Andre glanced at his watch and got to his feet. 'It is time for dinner,' he said, adding courteously, 'Papa hopes you will join us.' His brief smile did not reach his eyes. 'I think he wishes to talk about computers.'

She bit her lip. 'I hope you don't think I've been interfering.'

'*Au contraire*. It was Maman who insisted that the *domaine* must enter the computer age.' He shook his head ruefully. 'Since we lost her, I am aware that matters have been allowed to slide. But you seem to have persuaded him that we must move with the times. Permit me to thank you.' He added quietly, 'I hope when you return to England you will not feel your time here has been completely wasted.'

As she watched him go, it occurred to her that

they'd just taken the first step in the process of separation. Not a giant stride by any means, but a beginning.

But, she reminded herself, her throat tightening, it was also very clearly an ending.

The Baron was in an ebullient mood over the vegetable soup, the wonderfully garlicky roast lamb and the chocolate mousse. He had already, he said, contacted a computer firm in Dijon, and a representative would be visiting them to make his recommendations the following day.

'He believes that we should have what he calls a website,' he added, helping himself to cheese. 'You approve, *mademoiselle*?'

She said quickly, 'I think it's a wonderful idea.' As well as long overdue, she thought grimly, wondering how Mademoiselle Chaloux could have allowed matters to slip in this way.

'Ah, but I have not finished,' he said, and turned to Andre. '*Mon fils*, I have decided that this year we shall again celebrate the birthday of Baron Emile.'

Andre's brows lifted. 'Is it not a little late for that? We have less than a month to prepare.'

The Baron waved a hand. 'I have spoken with Gaston and Clothilde and they agree with me that his memory has been neglected for too long, and that all will go well.' He smiled at Ginny. 'Mademoiselle Mason will see the Château Terauze *en fête* and her presence will add grace to an already happy occasion.

'Tomorrow, I shall make a list of guests to be invited,' the Baron went on. 'And we must order cards to be printed. I remember my dear one always used the same company.' He nodded. 'I shall look in my desk for the name,' he announced and went off to do so, taking his coffee with him.

When they were alone, Andre said quietly, 'You know what I am going to ask, Virginie. I have not seen him so animated for a long time, and hope you can find it in your heart to indulge him by staying until the party.' He paused. 'And, although this may be no incentive, you will also have my gratitude.'

Gratitude, she thought. Will that stop me feeling as if I'm dying inside?

She stared down at the table. 'Then it seems I have little choice.'

She did not hear him leave the room, and it was only when she eventually looked up that she realised she was alone.

* * *

Only one more day, Ginny told herself as she walked back from the village. Then the most difficult three weeks of her life would be over and done with.

She paused to transfer Madame's canvas bag from one hand to the other. She had only bought a few vegetables, yet somehow it seemed infinitely heavier than usual.

Maybe she was just tired, she thought. She couldn't pretend she'd been sleeping well. The inner tensions of continuing to share a roof with Andre had seen to that.

Not that she encountered him that much, apart from mealtimes, and he'd invariably breakfasted before she got downstairs. His days were spent pruning the precious vines, while after dinner, more often than not, he would excuse himself courteously and disappear down to La Petite Maison to spend the evening, drinking and playing cards with Jules, or so Madame Rameau intimated with raised brows and pursed lips.

And, wherever he was, he was invariably accompanied by Barney, who had wholeheartedly transferred his devotion from the father to the son.

But if Andre thought he was being considerate

by keeping out of her way, he could not be more wrong, thought Ginny, stifling a sigh. She found herself constantly on tenterhooks, awaiting his return. Feeling her heart lift as the sudden buzz in the house heralded his return. Longing to look at him and see him drop the formal mask he now used in his dealings with her and smile.

She could cope in the daytime, becoming immersed in preparations for the party, from sending out the invitations—and being astounded at the acceptance rate—to even more practical matters such as helping to wash by hand the array of exquisite eighteenth-century porcelain plates and dishes and amazing sets of crystal which Gaston had reverently produced from a cupboard, to cleaning the elaborate silver candelabra which would stand down the centre of the long table in the hall.

And in the past twenty-four hours, she'd become Madame's kitchen assistant, helping prepare the fragrant hams, joints of beef, turkeys and game to be consumed by the guests.

Moreover, Madame's brother-in-law, a keen fisherman, had promised to supply enough perch and pike for a massive and traditional fish stew.

'And I shall show you, *mon enfant,* how to make

jambon persille,' Madame promised, referring with a satisfied nod to the famous Burgundian dish, resembling a mosaic of ham, shallots, garlic, wine and parsley.

The Baron, who had overheard, was amused. 'Clothilde guards her recipes with care, *mademoiselle.* You are honoured. Clearly you have the makings of a serious cook.'

Who will probably be living out of a microwave in the months to come, Ginny thought, murmuring an appropriate response.

And who was most certainly not the flavour of the month in another quarter.

Monique Chaloux's face had turned to stone when she'd arrived to find a computer engineer replacing the current system with a panoply of new hardware and software, and she had protested vigorously than it was an unnecessary expense, shooting a look at Ginny that spoke daggers.

But the Baron, having taken delivery of the latest thing in laptops for his personal use, was bullish about his decision, telling her that the real expense would be to lag behind their competitors. Adding blandly, to Ginny's horror, that if Monique had problems using the software, she could always ask

Mademoiselle Mason for her assistance, as he intended to do.

'But that is hardly fair,' Mademoiselle had said smoothly. 'To intrude on what remains of her time with us with such mundane matters.'

'On the contrary,' Ginny returned quietly. 'Monsieur le Baron knows I am happy to help. In this small way, to repay the kindness I've been shown here.'

And tried to pretend she had not seen Andre's ironic glance.

She had not intended to be at the party for all kinds of reasons, one being that she had no suitable outfit, and had planned to invent some illness, minor but enough to confine her to her room, on the day itself.

But Madame Rameau had removed one major obstacle by demanding to know what she intended to wear during one of their shopping expeditions, dismissing her faltering reply, and conducting her forthwith to a small shop in a side street, where, Ginny noticed with alarm, the window held just one silk blouse in an exquisite mélange of rainbow colours.

Inside, the proprietress, stunningly chic in grey, had looked her over, nodded and produced a whole armful of evening wear for her to try, in spite of Ginny's uneasy conviction that the price of anything on offer would easily exceed her modest resources.

There were two dresses, however, that immediately attracted her, a full length, long-sleeved ivory silk in Empire style, which she put aside with a pang of regret as altogether too bridal, and a gorgeous black taffeta, with a full skirt reaching just below the knee and a deep square neck against which her skin seemed to glow like pearl.

She couldn't see a price label anywhere, but when she asked diffidently about the cost, she found to her astonishment that it was half what she'd have expected, and therefore—just—affordable, especially as she already possessed an almost new pair of high-heeled black shoes.

Within minutes, the transaction was done and she was watching the taffeta dress being swathed in tissue paper and laid reverently in a blue and silver striped box tied up with ribbons.

As she carried it through the market, she'd felt momentarily like Cinderella, a dream soon shattered by the sound of Madame scolding a stall-holder over the price of leeks.

A much needed reality check, she thought ruefully now, as she climbed the final slope to the gates of the château, and one that she'd returned to over and over again in the days which followed.

She went in the back door and into the kitchen, where Jules was standing talking to his aunt. And just beyond them, lying on the kitchen table, Ginny saw two rabbits.

'*Bonjour, mademoiselle. Ça va?*' Jules greeted her cheerfully. He gestured at the rabbits. 'Tonight Tante Clothilde will cook them for you in her special mustard sauce.' He kissed his fingertips. '*Formidable.*'

Ginny stared at the rabbits, feeling curiously hollow as she unfastened her coat.

Fur, she thought. Ears and tails. That would have to be removed.

She said hoarsely, 'Where did they come from?'

'I shot them early this morning.' He sounded surprised. 'The noise of my gun did not disturb you?'

Mutely, Ginny shook her head, only to discover that was a serious mistake. Gagging suddenly, she dropped the bag of vegetables and ran to the scullery sink, where she was swiftly and unpleasantly sick.

As she straightened, the world still reeling around her, she was given a drink of water, then, firmly supported by Madame's sheltering arm, found herself guided out of the kitchen to the *petit salon,* where she was deposited on the sofa in front of the fire.

'I'm sorry,' Ginny whispered. 'It—it was seeing those rabbits. I'm not usually so squeamish.'

Madame nodded. 'But everything changes when one is *enceinte, mon enfant.'* She gave Ginny a re-assuring smile. 'And for tonight's dinner, I shall roast a chicken very simply.'

'*Enceinte,*' Ginny repeated numbly. 'You mean...'

'That you are to have a child, *petite.'*

'No—you must be mistaken.' *You have to be...*

Madame shook her head. 'I knew from the first. And Monsieur Andre will tell you that I am never wrong.'

Ginny stared up at her. 'You told him too?'

'That he was to be a father? Most certainly. It is important news for a man.' She patted Ginny on the shoulder. 'And another generation for the Châ-teau Terauze. It will bring great happiness.'

Happiness, thought Ginny when Madame had bustled off and she was alone. What possible hap-piness can come from being married to a man out of his sense of duty? And when there's someone more suitable waiting in the wings?

She closed her eyes and leaned back against the cushions. Falling in love with someone, knowing you wanted to spend your life making him happy should be a wonderful thing. Not like the wretchedness and desperation that were threatening to overwhelm her, but which must for ever remain her secret.

At least, she whispered silently, until I'm long gone from here, which must—must be soon.

CHAPTER ELEVEN

SHE HAD BRACED herself for Andre's arrival, but when he walked into the room and she saw the bleakness of his expression, her heart felt wrenched.

She said huskily, 'I'm sorry.'

And it was true. It was her misguided attempt to intervene in whatever was going on between Cilla and himself that had triggered this disaster. Instead, she should have closed her eyes and kept her distance.

Because she'd known from the start—probably from the moment she saw him—the danger she was in.

But she'd told herself that her feelings were down to dislike and resentment, too inexperienced to recognise the tug of sexual thrall for what it was. Or to realise that it was jealousy as well as anger that had taken her to him that day. And love that had brought her here.

He said abruptly, 'I too regret—everything.' He

shook his head. 'I have been hoping, praying that for once Clothilde might be wrong.'

She winced inwardly. 'But it doesn't change anything,' she said quickly. 'I shall still go back to England.'

His mouth hardened. '*Au contraire.* Tomorrow at the party I shall announce our engagement, and we will be married as soon as the legal formalities are complete.'

'No,' she said. 'You don't—you can't mean that.'

'You forget, Virginie.' His voice was harsh. 'I know what my father suffered, knowing his only child was being raised in another country by another man, and the extreme it drove him to. You think I will allow that to happen to me? That I would be content to provide financial support and the occasional visit?' He drew a sharp breath. 'Never in this world.'

'But you don't understand…'

'No,' he said grimly. 'It is you, *ma belle,* who cannot comprehend how I would feel if our child was sick or in an accident and I could not be with you at the bedside. Or the pain of not seeing that first step—hearing that first word.'

He paused. 'And whatever you may believe, there is still a stigma attached to a child born outside marriage. Bastard is an ugly word which some people do not hesitate to use. Almost from the moment she arrived back in Terauze, Maman had the support and protection of Papa Bertrand, but even so, she was not invulnerable.'

He added quietly, 'And nor was I.'

Ginny was silent, remembering from her own youth how cruel children could be, in her case, if you did not have the trendiest clothes, or if they found your school meals were subsidised. Imagining the kind of jibes that would have been levelled at the man looking at her so steadily.

He said, 'But who will defend you, Virginie? Your mother? I do not think so.'

Nor did she, all her attempts at making contact over the past weeks having totally failed, but, just the same, she lifted her chin defiantly. 'You're determined to think the worst of her.'

Andre shrugged. 'I wish you to face reality. And, in doing so, to accept the shelter of marriage for yourself and our baby. We should not forget that the child could be the future heir to Terauze.'

But marriage is the reality I can't bear to face, Ginny thought wildly.

Living with you, sleeping with you, needing you.

And, when you're not with me, wondering where you are and who you're with.

How can I do that? How can I—when the shelter you offer will only make me more vulnerable?

Her voice shook a little. 'Wouldn't it be better for this heir to be born in a marriage of love rather than convenience?'

'*Peut-être,*' he said. 'In an ideal world. But we must deal with the situation as it is.'

He walked over to the sofa and knelt, taking her hand. 'Virginie, I beg you honour me by becoming my wife.' He added with constraint, 'I promise I will try to make you happy.'

At the expense of someone else's sorrow...

She thought it, but did not say it. She looked at the tanned fingers enclosing her own, and nodded reluctantly.

'Then I suppose—yes.' She released her hand from his clasp. 'I—I don't know how to fight you any more, Andre.'

He smiled at her and rose. '*Vraiment?* Then you will make the perfect wife, *ma mie.* Now I shall tell Papa Bertrand the good news.'

'All of it?' she asked apprehensively.

He shrugged again. '*Pourquoi pas?*' he countered. 'If he has not guessed already.'

He bent and, realising he intended to kiss her and unable to trust herself not to respond, she shrank back against the cushions.

He straightened, the firm mouth twisting in derision. 'Keep your distance by day, if you wish, *chérie.* But the nights will bring their own compensations.' He walked to the door and turned. 'For us both,' he added softly. 'As I am sure you remember.'

And left her staring after him, her heart beating wildly.

The black taffeta, Ginny decided critically, surveying herself in the mirror, looked almost better tonight than it had done in the shop, which was gratifying when this might be the only occasion she'd be able to wear it. And her high-heeled court shoes and sheer black tights somehow made her slim legs look endless.

It was a long time since she'd been to a big party and even longer since she'd possessed a dress quite as flattering and—well, sexy as this one, and, in spite of her very real concerns about the future, she felt a flutter of excitement inside her.

I've scrubbed up pretty well, she thought, reverting to self-mockery. Tonight I might even have given Cilla a run for her money.

She'd phoned both Rosina and her sister the previous day, telling them that she was to be married, but, again, her messages went straight to voice-mail, and there had been no call-back. Yet surely they couldn't still be in the Seychelles.

It's as if I've ceased to exist for them, she acknowledged with a faint sigh as she went downstairs.

The table in the centre of the hall was now laden with food and lit by candelabra. In a corner, a group of local musicians were quietly tuning up, and two girls from the village, resplendent in brief dark skirts with crisp white shirts and aprons were waiting to serve drinks.

Gaston, checking that all was ready, gave her his warm, shy smile and told her that the Baron and Monsieur Andre were in the *salon.*

The door was ajar and as Ginny paused to smooth her skirt and take a deep breath, she heard the Baron say, 'You expect me to be pleased? To accept this girl as your wife, when I hoped that for you, *mon fils,* it would be a very different marriage.'

And Andre's reply, 'Papa, it is the best I can hope for. And I have only myself to blame.'

For one numb, stricken moment, Ginny stood motionless. Her overwhelming temptation was to retreat to her room, pack her things and disappear into the night.

But that would be the coward's way out, as well as disrupting an important night for the Château Terauze, when Andre went in search of her, as he undoubtedly would.

Besides, she told herself, she already knew and accepted how things were and it would be sheer hypocrisy to pretend otherwise and throw any kind of wobbly, so she pushed the door wide and walked in, her head held high and her smile firmly pinned in place.

They both turned to look at her, but the Baron was the first to speak. '*Ravissante,*' he declared, forcing a smile. 'Is that not so, Andre?'

There was the briefest silence, and she saw Andre's mouth twist almost wryly. He said quietly, '*Tu as raison, mon père.* You are—very lovely, Virginie.'

She murmured an awkward word of thanks and turned away, feeling the colour rise in her face.

After all, she thought, what else could he say?

It was marginally easier when people began to arrive, and all she had to do was stand between Andre and his father, smiling and saying '*Bonsoir,*' as one introduction succeeded another in quick succession.

I hope I don't have to answer questions later on who I've met tonight, she thought, as the faces began to merge into a blur.

When the last guests had arrived, she managed to detach herself from Andre, enmeshed in a discussion with other *vignerons,* and find a quiet corner in which to draw breath.

But, almost at once, she found herself accosted by Monique Chaloux in dark green brocade.

'One would hardly recognise you, *mademoiselle.* What a difference expensive clothes can make.'

'I wouldn't know,' Ginny returned coolly. 'I can't afford such pleasures.'

Mademoiselle's eyes narrowed. 'Yet you are wearing a Louise Vernier tonight. A present from Monsieur Andre, perhaps, to pay you for whatever services you have provided, before he sends you on your way?' She tittered. 'He has been generous, so you cannot be as dull as you seem in bed.'

'How dare you?' Ginny said, her voice shaking. 'I paid for this dress myself.'

'You have two thousand euros to squander? Permit me to doubt it.'

'Two thousand?' Ginny stared at her. 'You're being ridiculous. It cost less than two hundred.'

'No,' Monique said cuttingly. 'If you believe that, you are the fool, *mademoiselle*. But Monsieur Andre will soon tire of you, so enjoy your good fortune while you may.'

She moved away, leaving Ginny trembling from a mix of emotions in which anger predominated.

When Andre appeared at her side, she said furiously, 'Did you really pay for this dress?'

His brows lifted. 'Ah,' he said. 'I wondered why *notre chère* Monique had sought you out. How good of her to tell you.'

'Then it's true.' She took a deep breath. 'How could I have been stupid enough to think I could afford even a handkerchief in that shop?' She glared up at him. 'For two pins, I'd take the dress off and throw it at you.'

'Then it is fortunate I do not have two pins,' he returned, the faint amusement in his voice doing nothing to placate her. 'At least not at this moment because we have an announcement to make.' He took her hand and led her through the laughter and talk of the party to the little rostrum built to accommodate the band.

'*Messieurs et mesdames.*' At the sound of his voice a hush fell on the room. 'You joined us tonight to remember the anniversary of the Baron Emile, but I have another cause to celebrate. To my great joy, Mademoiselle Mason—Virginie— has consented to be my wife. I present—the future Baronne de Terauze.'

There was a concerted gasp, then applause rang out as the Baron stepped forward, beaming, and proffered a flat velvet case. Inside, shimmering with crimson fire, lay the ruby necklace from the portrait in the *salon,* and the guests clapped and cheered as Andre fastened the jewels round Ginny's throat, before bending to kiss her hand and her lips.

She stood in the curve of his arm, forcing herself to smile in response to all this goodwill. As she and Andre stepped down from the rostrum, they were immediately surrounded by well-wishers offering handshakes and embraces, with one exception. Over the heads of the crowd, Ginny saw Monique standing by the wall, her face a mask of fury and disbelief.

Resolutely dismissing the image from her mind,

she let Andre guide her through the throng, his hands lightly clasping her waist, pausing now and then to receive congratulations and boisterous good wishes.

At the same time, she found herself wondering wistfully how it would have been if Andre had indeed been marrying her for love.

Gaston's announcement that the food was being served managed to divert everyone's attention and, while plates were being filled, Ginny found Andre once more at her side.

He touched the rubies glowing round her throat, saying softly, 'They were made for you, *mignonne*,' before allowing his fingers to drift down to where the first swell of her breasts lifted above her low neckline.

'Just as you, *ma belle*, were made for me.' He bent forward, his breath fanning her ear as he whispered, 'Sleep with me tonight, Virginie. Let me know that you belong to me.'

His face seemed strained, his gaze oddly intense. He said again, 'Virginie…'

The swift hammer of her heart was half-joyous, half-fearful. She wanted so badly to say yes and know that, for an hour or two, he would belong to her too, lost in the exchanges of sexual pleasure.

But with the added danger that she might so easily be betrayed into saying what he did not want to hear—and what must for ever remain unspoken. The words, I love you.

But as she hesitated, she heard the loud clang of a bell and saw a surprised Gaston hastening to the front door.

She saw the candles flare in the sudden draught as the door opened to admit the late arrival. Through the shifting mass of people, she saw a woman, her mass of blonde hair spilling on to her shoulders as she pulled off her woollen cap. For a moment, she thought it must be Dominique Lavaux, who had not replied to her invitation, but then, above the buzz of conversation, she heard a voice she knew all too well, announcing autocratically, 'I'm here to see my sister, Virginia Mason. Where is she, please?'

She stood, numb with disbelief, as Cilla, in her violet quilted coat, came pushing her way through the crowd towards her. But only to walk past as if she was invisible.

'Oh, Andre.' There was a note of hysteria in Cilla's voice. 'I had to come, because everything's just awful and I don't know what to do.'

And with a strangled sob, she threw herself

straight at Andre, burying her face in his shirt front as he caught her.

For a moment there was total, astonished silence. Then Jules appeared from nowhere with a chair. He detached the weeping girl from Andre with cool authority, made her sit, and when his aunt arrived with brandy, encouraged her firmly to drink.

It occurred to Ginny, suddenly transformed into helpless bystander, that this was one party no one would forget in a hurry. Least of all herself.

She stepped forward into the breach. Raising her voice, she said in her clear schoolgirl French, 'Madame Rameau, would you have the goodness to prepare a room for my sister. She has had a long and tiresome journey and needs rest.'

Madame gave the drooping beauty an old-fashioned look, but nodded and bustled off.

Ginny walked over to the chair and put a hand on her sister's shoulder. 'Has Mother come with you? Is she waiting somewhere?'

'Mother?' Cilla reared up, nearly spilling what was left of the brandy. 'You must be joking. She's turned me out and won't even speak to me—not since Jon broke off our engagement. Why else would I be here?'

Why indeed? thought Ginny. Conscious of the

eyes and ears around them and Baron Bertrand's shocked face, she said, 'We'll talk about this later. Why don't I take you upstairs to freshen up in my bathroom?'

'Your bathroom?' Cilla seemed to focus on her for the first time, her eyes narrowing as she spotted the rubies. 'What's going on here? What's the celebration?'

Ginny kept her voice steady. 'Among other things, my engagement to Andre.'

'Engagement,' Cilla repeated. Her laugh was breathless as she looked back at Andre, who was standing stony-faced, his arms folded. 'Is this a joke?'

'*Au contraire, madame.*' It was Jules who spoke. 'The marriage of our future Baron is a serious affair, but also a time of great happiness for the Château Terauze.'

Cilla got to her feet. 'But I thought,' she began, then paused, swaying slightly, a hand to her head, as she whispered, 'Andre...'

Then, as Andre took one slow step towards her, Jules again intervened. 'You are clearly not yourself, *mademoiselle.* You must allow me to assist you.'

And before anything more could be said or done,

he calmly lifted Cilla into his arms and carried her across the room and up the stairs, leaving an amazed silence behind him.

'Did you expect this to happen?' Andre asked harshly. 'You received some advance warning, perhaps?'

They were in the *petit salon,* the last guests having left half an hour before and the Baron having bade them a tactful goodnight.

Although there'd been no mass exodus from the party, Cilla's arrival had changed the whole atmosphere of the evening, offering another sensation for the participants to mull over.

And, in private, a different confrontation.

'No,' Ginny protested. 'Of course not. I told my mother we were getting married, but I thought she was simply ignoring it like all my other messages. And clearly, she hasn't told Cilla.'

He said icily, 'But what irony, *n'est-ce pas,* that on the night of our engagement, your sister arrives to say her relationship with Monsieur Welburn is at an end.'

'Why do you say that?'

'Because *le bon* Jonathan is now free to choose again. You may regret even more our afternoon of delight.'

And what about you? she thought, stung by the note of derision in his voice. Everyone in the room saw you take that step towards her. If Jules hadn't butted in, I'd have had to watch you carrying her up the stairs.

When, only minutes before, you'd been asking me to sleep with you...

Because it's obvious why she's come here, she thought, and it's not to see me.

She said, 'And you may be reading too much into a lovers' tiff brought on by pre-wedding stress. It happens.'

'But not, I think, in this case.' He paused. 'You will be speaking to her?'

'In the morning. She's had a cup of *bouillon*, followed by one of Madame's *tisanes* so I've been instructed to let her sleep.'

He nodded. 'Clothilde is very wise.' He added quietly, 'We all need to sleep. Everything will be different tomorrow.'

Everything has changed already...

Including the rubies that now seemed to resemble drops of blood against her skin.

She reached to the back of her neck, fumbling for the clasp. 'I should return these. I expect they belong in a safe somewhere.'

'Permit me.'

Ginny tried not to flinch as he dealt with the awkward fastening, the brush of his fingers against her nape a brief but telling agony.

'You can manage your dress?'

'Oh, yes.' Her response and involuntary recoil were both too hasty, as she was reminded of how the night might have ended. Of the taffeta slipping to the floor with a rustle like autumn leaves as Andre undressed her. His hands lingering in erotic persuasion as he explored her naked flesh.

Let me know that you belong to me.

At least she hadn't said yes to him, with all the hideous embarrassment that would have led to under the circumstances. But being spared such an aftermath was no real consolation, although perhaps that too would seem different in the morning.

She thought, I can only hope.

She summoned a travesty of a smile. 'Well— goodnight.'

He was already turning away. '*Bonsoir,* Virginie, *et dors bien.*'

Nodding jerkily, she headed for the door. Walked without hurrying to the stairs and climbed them steadily. Then began to run, as if pursued by demons, to the room that was still nominally hers and closed the door on her fragmenting world.

'Oh, it's you,' said Cilla listlessly. She was reclining against her pillows looking enchanting in a low-cut blue silk nightdress trimmed with lace, a tray holding a barely touched breakfast on the bed beside her.

No amount of designer dresses could ever turn me into competition for her, Ginny thought with a pang. She moved the tray and sat down.

'Not hungry?'

Cilla shrugged. 'Not for bread and jam. Is that all that passes for breakfast round here?'

'Pretty much, although you can have *croissants* or *pains au chocolat* if you ask before the trip to the *boulangerie*. And there are eggs, of course.' Ginny tried a smile. 'I've just fed the hens.'

'Aren't there servants to do that? The woman who gave me that revolting drink last night, for instance.' Cilla shuddered. 'I thought she was trying to poison me, and this morning she turns up with breakfast. No wonder I have no appetite.'

Ginny said quietly, 'What's gone wrong, Cilly-Billy? I mean between you and Jon?'

Cilla's head lifted sharply at the idiotic childhood

nickname. But instead of delivering the expected blast, she seemed to be fighting tears.

She said huskily, 'Nothing that wasn't already a problem. But I suppose going to the Seychelles brought it all to a head. It was only when we were on the plane that I found Mother had deliberately left the phones behind, so we couldn't be contacted. "Bothered with stupid questions" was how she put it. When we got to the hotel, I tried to call Jon, but his mother answered and I knew she'd only give me a hard time, so I hung up. After all, she's never liked me, and finding that I'm penniless hasn't helped one bit.'

She added bleakly, 'I should have left him to you, but Jon was the catch of the neighbourhood, as Mother never failed to point out. And, to be honest, I fancied being lady of the manor and living in that beautiful house.'

'What I didn't want was the endless talk about horses and farming and Lady Welburn's lectures on gardening, and the importance of a good mulch. And certainly not for the rest of my life.'

'You can't mean that,' Ginny protested.

'Actually, I do.' Cilla played with the embroidered edge of the sheet. 'The Seychelles gave me time to think, and I realised that if Jon was my one true love, I'd never have simply gone off like that—or done a lot of other things either. So I was all set to suggest we should think again. Only he beat me to it.'

She chewed at her lip. 'You see, I paid Andre a visit at his hotel one afternoon, and one of the chambermaids saw me leaving his room. By the time I got back, the word had spread as far as Welburn Manor.

'Jon came right out with it. Demanded I tell him what had happened.' She shrugged. 'And I said, "Wouldn't you like to know?" and handed back his ring.

'So I had to tell Mother,' she added wryly. 'And then all the real hell broke loose.'

She shuddered. 'She started screaming at me, telling me I must be insane. That I'd humiliated her in front of the entire neighbourhood, and she'd never forgive me. That I could starve in the gutter because there wasn't a chance in hell of her letting me scrounge off her, or saddling Howard with me either.'

Ginny's head was spinning, but she managed to ask, 'Who is Howard?'

'The man she met playing bridge at our hotel. Quiet, quite nice-looking, living in Hampstead and all set to be our next stepfather. Or mine, anyway,' she added. 'I don't think she's mentioned you.'

'But she's only just been widowed,' said Ginny. 'Does he know that?'

'Don't be silly. She spotted him and had him attached to her side before the end of the first week. She's quite an operator, our ma.

'And, of course, this time the marriage will have no strings attached because he has a son and heir already.'

'What do you mean?'

Cilla shrugged again. 'Apparently she and Andrew had an agreement. He wanted a legitimate heir. She promised she could provide him with one. But she'd had a bad time when I was born, and somehow persuaded her doctor to perform some procedure to ensure she'd never get pregnant again. A "tubal ligation", she called it. She thought that she could fob Andrew off with some excuse for her failure to produce, but eventually he insisted they both had tests, and the truth came out.'

Ginny drew a sharp breath. 'Oh, my God. He must have told Andre and that's why he called her a cheat.'

'But she didn't see it like that,' said Cilla. 'She wanted money and comfort, so, to her, the end justified the means. It still does, because I don't think she's any more in love with Howard than she was with Andrew.'

She glanced round the spacious, pretty room. 'After all, you seem to have fallen on your feet,' she commented with acerbity. 'Who would have thought it?'

Ginny bit her lip and rose. 'I'm sorry you've had such a difficult time, but I'm sure Mother will come round eventually. In the meantime, I'm sure Andre will let you remain with us while you sort out your future.'

'Oh, I know that already,' Cilla said, smiling up at her with a kind of lazy contentment, her eyes shining. 'He visited me earlier—so sweet of him—and said I could stay as long as I wanted. So that's all right.'

Ginny nodded and headed for the door, where she turned, longing to leave but impelled to speak.

Her voice shook a little. 'Cilla, tell me, please. What did happen in Andre's hotel room that afternoon?'

Her sister's smile deepened to mockery. 'Wouldn't you like to know,' she said.

And she began to laugh as Ginny, feeling sick, stumbled from the room.

CHAPTER TWELVE

As THE LONG, agonisingly slow days passed into weeks, Ginny began to feel that she'd become a bystander in her own life, watching helplessly from a distance as Cilla morphed into the role of Andre's future wife.

It was achieved with great charm and an eagerness to learn she had never displayed before. Baron Bertrand, having recovered from the shock of her arrival, was now openly indulgent. Even Madame Rameau, inclined at first to eye the newcomer askance, had been won over and was actually teaching Cilla the basics of cooking.

She'd pretty much taken over the daily shopping too, Ginny watching and listening in envious admiration as Cilla chatted away to the shopkeepers and stallholders in what seemed to be flawless French, courtesy, of course, of her stay at that exclusive establishment in Switzerland.

At other times, she was immersing herself in every aspect of the life of the *domaine*, displaying

what seemed to be a genuine interest in the complex production of fine wines, and spending several hours a day among the vines or in the *chai*.
Discussing what she had learned in the evening,
over the dinner table.

As I never did, Ginny acknowledged unhappily.
Because I told myself that it was dangerous to become too involved. That to do so would only make
it harder to say goodbye when the time came.

So I can hardly start asking questions now, not
without appearing jealous, which would embarrass
me and everyone else. Especially Andre.

They were still, she supposed, officially engaged
to be married, but an engagement could easily be
ended as Cilla had demonstrated, particularly as
the wedding itself had not been mentioned since
the night of the fete.

On the few occasions when she found herself
alone with Andre, the only topic of conversation,
raised quietly and politely, was her health.

'Clothilde tells me you are still being sick,' he'd
commented recently.

'As soon as I wake up each morning,' she'd
returned ruefully. 'I could almost set my watch by
it.' She paused. 'But she tells me it will stop very
soon.'

His brief smile was wintry. 'I am glad to hear it for your sake.' And left her.

What he never mentioned was that other early morning when he'd told Cilla she could stay. Leaving Ginny free to guess at what else might have been said. To guess and, accordingly, to suffer...

Nor had he ever expressed, by word or look, the slightest interest in sleeping with her again. Instead he was spending his nights at La Petite Maison. Probably not alone.

But she did not let herself think about that, concentrating instead on how the problem of her expected baby could be resolved. What happened when a man fathered a child by a girl he no longer wanted? After all, he could hardly expect his new bride to raise another woman's child, especially when the mother was her own sister.

It was an impossible situation and she quailed at its implications.

The most equitable solution, she supposed, would be for Andre to allow her to return to England as she'd requested so often in the past and have the baby there. He was, she knew, too honourable to stint on financial support, and she could work part-time until the child was of school age.

And if her mother was truly planning to remarry

with such scandalous haste and live in London, maybe she could occupy the empty Keeper's Cottage in Rosina's place.

According to her most recent letter from Mrs Pel, who'd become a regular correspondent, her mother's absence as well as Cilla's broken engagement was still providing ample sustenance for the local gossips. And the new regime at the café had not found favour with the customers, who were staying away in droves. 'I'm told Iris Potter is thinking of selling up,' she wrote.

I suppose I could revert to Plan A, Ginny thought with a sigh. Take another shot at becoming the new Miss Finn.

But wherever she went and whatever she did, it seemed likely that Andre would want to establish and maintain contact with his child and some kind of regular access would have to be agreed, however painful she would find it.

And repeating over and over again that she only had herself to blame did nothing to dispel the growing desolation that haunted her.

The attitude of Monique Chaloux only added to her wretchedness. 'The little sister,' she'd exclaimed effusively. '*Quelle enchanteresse. Quelle jolie blonde.* No wonder all the men, including

Monsieur Andre, have been rendered *bouleversé* by her presence.'

'No wonder indeed,' Ginny agreed expressionlessly, aware that Mademoiselle's goading remarks were almost certainly intended to punish her for having introduced the new computer system which Monique had still failed to master.

In a way, Ginny was almost grateful for the constant errors that had to be corrected, the deletions needing to be painstakingly retrieved, the data assigned to the wrong files or even omitted altogether.

After all, apart from occasionally walking Barney, she had little else to occupy her. And at least putting the mistakes right gave Ginny a sense of purpose and stopped her brooding, as well as improving her own computer skills, something which, she told herself resolutely, would stand her in good stead for the future. Back in England. Alone.

But, in turn, she struggled to understand the labyrinthine filing system of Mademoiselle's devising which seemed, in some inexplicable way, to swallow up letters, invoices and bank statements, never to be traced again. So maybe the end result was a draw, she told herself with a shrug, quelling the odd feeling of uneasiness which could be ascribed to any number of causes.

Including the understandably strained atmosphere at the château.

So when a spell of fine spring weather led to Andre's suggestion that they should undertake the delayed visit to Beaune, she agreed without hesitation, even if the trip was more for Cilla's pleasure than her own.

After the peace of Terauze, the sudden confluence of busy main roads with large lorries thundering past as they neared their destination came as something of a shock to the system, but this was soon forgotten as Ginny caught her first sight of Beaune, sheltered securely by its striking medieval walls.

'Oh, it's gorgeous,' she exclaimed impulsively as Andre turned through an arched gateway into a labyrinth of narrow streets, and saw him smile.

'That was also the opinion of your *beau-père* when I brought him here,' he said, slotting the car neatly into an empty parking space. 'Now we shall walk a little. Nothing is too far away.'

He guided them both through another maze of quaint, cosy streets into a square dominated by a massive building, a spire rising above its forbidding stone walls.

Is this where they dispose of unwanted visitors? Ginny wondered mordantly as they crossed to an entrance made no more cheerful by the massive door knocker depicting a salamander eating a fly.

Will you come into my parlour? she chanted under her breath. And took a step into a different world. One that stopped her in her tracks, gasping with a delight as wholehearted as it was unexpected as she found herself in a cobbled courtyard, staring at one of the most amazing buildings she'd ever seen in her life.

It was clearly very old, its creamy stones almost golden in the early spring sunlight, but it was the colourful design that entranced her, from the slender pillars of the arcade that supported the ornate upper balcony up to the beautiful dormer windows.

And above them the kind of roof she'd never seen before, its tiles glazed and geometrically patterned in spectacular green, rust and black against a golden background, with gilded weathervanes soaring towards the sky.

She turned to Andre. 'What in the world is this place?' Her voice was husky.

'The Hotel-Dieu, built six centuries ago by Nicholas Rolin, Philippe le Bon's Chancellor, as a hospital for the poor.' His mouth twisted. 'Perhaps, as the King of France remarked, to make amends for all those he'd helped to impoverish. Whatever Rolin's motives, it has become a symbol of our region, its decoration reminding Burgundians of their Flemish roots.'

'Is it still a hospital?'

'No, a museum. The sick and elderly were moved to modern buildings some forty years ago. But all of them, including the Hotel-Dieu, are still maintained by the Hospices de Beaune charity which Nicholas and his wife established.'

Ginny looked back with awe at the astonishing façade. 'That must take some doing.'

Andre shook his head. 'Not when the charity owns some of the greatest vineyards in Burgundy. And in November, during the Trois Glorieuses, their new vintages are sold by auction to buyers from all over the world, raising five to six million euros.'

'Is that when they light the candle and have to bid before it burns out?' asked Cilla eagerly.

He grinned. 'No, that is only for the most important lot—La Pièce de Presidents—usually with a celebrity auctioneer encouraging the feeding frenzy.'

Cilla sighed. 'Oh, I would love to be there and see that.'

Andre said quietly, 'Then all you need do is stay here. You know the choice is yours.'

Ginny had the oddest sensation that the brightness of the day had faded as she watched him look down gravely and searchingly into her sister's upturned face. As she saw the exquisite, brilliant colour rise in her cheeks, and heard her murmur something shy, confused, and most un-Cilla-like before she turned away.

Because she knew all that shy radiance could mean only one thing.

That this time Cilla was genuinely and deeply in love.

And glancing at Andre, she saw him smile with quiet, dccp satisfaction as he led the way into the Hotel-Dieu and felt her heart turn over in agony.

The interior was just as astonishing and, under other circumstances, Ginny would have revelled in the history of the place, from the neat alcove bedrooms of the Great Hall, all facing towards the painted woodcarving of Christ on the altar at the end of the long room to the enormous painting of the Last Judgement in the tapestried *salle* specially built to house it.

But now I have to make my own judgement, she thought wryly, pain building inside her as she obediently studied the immense detail of the painting through one of the magnifying glasses supplied to visitors as if her life depended on it.

I know it can never be right to wreck three lives, she thought, so I must be the one to leave, even if I am condemning myself to a hell of regret. But will that be any worse than being with a man who has only married me out of duty?

Yes, Cilla will be shocked and hurt when she finds out about the baby, as she eventually must, but, loving him, she'll surely forgive him. And loving her, he'll stay faithful in future. And they'll be happy together.

I have to believe that. Have to…

When, at last, they re-emerged into the sunlight, Ginny, still wretchedly preoccupied with her bleak thoughts, took a clumsy step and stumbled on the cobbles.

'Fais attention, ma mie.' Andre was beside her, taking her hand, his arm encircling her in support. A simple action, but it sent a shiver of uncontrol-

lable, unbearable response reverberating through every nerve-ending in her body.

'Leave me alone.' Her voice was hoarse as she wrenched herself free.

She saw the shock in his dark face deepening to a kind of anguish, and realised Cilla was watching them, her eyes widening in the tingling silence. Knew she needed to pass the whole thing off, and quickly.

She even managed a little laugh. 'I'm sorry. You—you startled me.'

'*Evidemment.*' His own voice was quietly toneless. 'I too am—very sorry.'

Simple words, thought Ginny, as she picked her way with care to the gate. But, at the same time, they encompassed the entire situation. And drew a final line beneath it.

She wanted to be alone, to tend her wounds, and make her plans, but as that was impossible, she decided, instead, to play the tourist, and make the most of her final hours in Burgundy.

Before my own candle burns down and goes out, she thought, bracing herself against the wretchedness twisting inside her.

By the time they returned to Terauze, Ginny's face ached with smiling, and her throat was hoarse from the bright, interested questions she'd made herself ask.

Her worst moment had come in the Musée des Beaux Arts, when she'd turned impulsively to comment on the Turner-esque landscapes of an artist called Felix Ziem, only to see Cilla, close to Andre and looking up at him, her hand on his arm.

After that she'd concentrated feverishly on things she was meant to see and nothing else.

She'd already realised that although Andre's parents were English, he had become a true son of Burgundy, committed heart and soul to this ancient and historic region and its great wines.

And now clearly committed to selling the complete package of a future here with him to the girl he loved. It resounded passionately in every word he spoke.

And if only he'd been saying it to me, she whispered to herself in silent anguish as they drove back to Terauze, remembering how Cilla had hung on his every word.

At the château, Gaston was waiting. 'Your father wishes to see you, Monsieur Andre.' He added in a voice of doom, 'Monsieur Labordier and Monsieur Dechesnes are here.'

Andre swore under his breath. 'I will come at

once.' He turned to Ginny. 'We need to talk. To begin with, there is something you need to be told—about Lucille.'

Who had, Ginny noted, prudently disappeared kitchenwards.

'That won't be necessary.' She lifted her chin. 'I'm not blind or stupid and I'm well aware what's been going on. It's hardly the year's best-kept secret. However, I—I'd prefer not to discuss it.'

His mouth tightened. 'I realise it has been a shock. *Tout de même,* I had hoped for a more gracious response from you, Virginie.'

'Perhaps I'll think of one, eventually.' Sick at heart and afraid of giving too much away, she turned from him. 'Now I'm going to rest in my room.' *If it's still mine...*

Upstairs, she took off her coat and shoes and lay down on the bed, staring up at the ceiling, trying to empty her mind, to relax and let her genuine tiredness take over.

But that was not destined to happen any time soon, for just as she was beginning to drift, there was a tap on the door. Propping herself on one elbow, she saw Cilla peeping in at her.

'Oh,' she said. 'I was afraid you might be asleep.' She came nervously across to the bed and sat down on its edge. 'I—I've just had a word with Andre,' she went on, her tone constricted. 'And he's told me how you feel. But Ginny—please believe I didn't come to Terauze to fall in love. In fact, it's the last thing in the world I ever expected to happen. I never knew I could feel like this. I—I still can't believe it myself.'

Her smile was forced—apprehensive. 'And I'm sure you think it's too soon, and it won't last. But I know he's the only man I'll ever truly want and need, so can't you please—please try to be happy for me?'

'Ginny, I've had a bad dream. Can I get into bed with you?'

'Ginny, I've lost my pocket money. Will you buy me some sweets?'

'Ginny—don't tell Mummy I broke the jug.'

Words from the distant past echoed and re-echoed in Ginny's mind, reminding her of the vulnerable, dependent child who'd preceded the spoilt beauty. The little girl who'd believed that anything that went wrong could easily be put right. And who relied on her big sister to do it for her.

She thought, I was all she had...

She bit her lip hard. 'Of course I'll be happy for

you, Cilly-Billy,' she said, after a pause. 'It—just takes some getting used to. That's all.'

She smiled up with an effort. 'And now I really would like to relax. All that sightseeing seems to have knocked me out.'

Cilla nodded and rose. She looked down at Ginny, her lips puckering in faint anxiety.

She said in a rush, 'But it could happen for you too, Ginny. You could fall in love—if you'd only let yourself. I'm sure of it.'

Ginny kept smiling. 'Perhaps we're not all that lucky.'

Alone again, she turned over and lay like a stone, her face buried in the pillow. And whispered again, 'That's all.'

It was a real struggle not to weep her heart out for all she had lost.

Except it had not been lost. Because she'd thrown it away by refusing to face the truth that she was in love with him, and always had been.

Probably from that first moment. And why could she see that so clearly now—when it was all too late?

But she was glad she'd won the battle with her tears when, barely ten minutes later, her door was thrown open and Andre strode in.

She sat up, staring at him. 'I thought you had visitors.'

'They have gone.'

'And I said I did not want a discussion.'

'Nevertheless, there must be one.' His face was set and grim. 'And about our own future rather than that of Lucille.'

As if there could be any difference...

She met his gaze. 'Whereas I say that you and I have no future. That we should cut our losses and go our separate ways.'

'Separate?' He almost spat the word. 'How can that be when we are for ever linked by the child you are carrying? When...' He stopped, shaking his head.

Her throat tightened. 'I—I've no idea. I only know that I can't stay here. That you must let me go. And the sooner the better.'

There was a silence, then he said quietly, 'I can no longer argue against that. There are details to be settled, *naturellement,* which my lawyer, Henri Dechesnes, will discuss with you.'

And as he was here earlier, no doubt most of the discussion has already taken place...

She nodded. 'That would probably be best.' She

added jerkily, 'Don't worry, Andre. I won't ask for very much.'

His voice was ragged with sudden bitterness. 'You do not have to tell me that, Virginie. *Je crois bien.* And I was a fool ever to think—ever to hope for more.'

He paused. 'I shall go now and tell my father what has been decided.'

She steadied her voice. 'I'm sure he already knows—and will think we've made absolutely the right choices.'

'*Au contraire,* I am certain he will be deeply disappointed in us both, and will say so over dinner.'

She said quickly, 'Which would hardly be fair on Cilla. So, perhaps you'll make my excuses—and ask Clothilde to bring me some soup up here.'

'*D'accord*—if that is what you want.'

No, she thought, as he walked to the door. It is not what I want. But everything I truly wish must remain my secret until I'm out of here. And probably for ever.

CHAPTER THIRTEEN

GINNY AWOKE WITH a start, and lay for a moment wondering what had disturbed her.

She had not expected to sleep at all, yet it seemed she had done so, and deeply, because her supper tray, delivered with chilling disapproval by an unsmiling Madame Rameau, had been removed at some point without her being aware of it.

It was still early, but a persistent sense of restless unease drove her out of bed and across to the window to open the shutters on another cloudless blue sky lit by a misty sun.

She had not believed, that first morning, that she would ever find the view of the vines so appealing, or how quick she would be to see how they changed with the passing weeks. Or how much she would miss them. Miss everything, she thought. And everyone.

At present, the sap was rising, making the branches look as if they were weeping. Not that she'd seen it for herself, of course. It was one of the pieces of information that Cilla had acquired and eagerly passed on.

When she came to dress, after her shower, she found she was wrestling with the zip on her jeans, a discovery adding to her woes but spurring her into action at the same time.

I need to go online, she told herself. Now, while I have the house to myself. Find out about flights back to the UK. Jump before I'm pushed.

As she made her way up to the office, she became aware of an unfamiliar noise. A vague but persistent whine of machinery in swift bursts, getting louder as she mounted the winding stairs.

The office door was slightly open. She pushed it wider and saw Monique Chaloux on her knees, feverishly feeding sheet after sheet of paper into the shredder, oblivious to the fact that she was being watched.

But she shouldn't even be here, Ginny thought, startled. This isn't one of her days. And that stuff she's shredding looks like bank statements.

So what on earth's going on?

She said quietly, '*Bonjour, mademoiselle. Ça va?*'

The older woman glanced up, her face as white as the paper she was destroying. She was far from her usual *soignée* self. Her clothes looked as if they had been thrown on and her hair needed washing.

'You,' she said, almost spitting the word. 'What are you doing here?'

Ginny walked forward, raising her eyebrows. 'I think that should be my question.'

'And my own business,' Monique retorted. 'You are not mistress here yet.'

'Nor are these working hours,' Ginny said levelly. 'So who authorised you to destroy these documents and why?' She saw Monique hesitated, and bent, dragging the shredder's plug out of the wall socket. 'I'd like some answers.'

'You would like. You would like.' Mademoiselle's voice was harsh and jeering. 'What are you? Nothing but an interfering English bitch like that other one. Just as pale, just as dull.'

She got clumsily to her feet and even across the room Ginny could see she was shaking.

'I believed she was my friend, but instead I had to watch while she took the man I loved. Even when she went away, he could not forget her, and when she came back, *enceinte* with another man's baby, he married her. *C'etait incroyable.*'

Her voice rose. 'He should have loved me. I could

have given him children of his own, not the leavings of some *Anglais.*

'When she died, I thought I had been given another chance. So I returned, hoping that at last he would see me as the wife he should have taken.'

She gave a strident bitter laugh. 'And he was grateful to me, *ah, oui,* and kind. All these years, so grateful and so kind. Until the night of Baron Emile's birthday when I saw Andre fasten the Baronne's rubies round your throat, and I knew then I had wasted my life in vain hope.

'I realised that I would have to see another *putaine Anglaise* in the place that should have been mine, and once again I would leave Terauze with nothing.'

She shook her head, a trace of spittle on her rigidly smiling lips. 'But not this time.' She looked down at the remaining papers crushed in her hand. 'All these years of devotion deserve a generous reward from the Duchards and I have taken it.'

Ginny stiffened. My God, she thought. She's been stealing money. Maybe those computer glitches were deliberate. A cover-up. If so, this is real trouble. And I'm not just uneasy. I'm beginning to be scared.

She said quietly, 'I'm sure Baron Bertrand truly

values you, *mademoiselle.'* She paused. 'So why don't I go and find him, so you can talk things over.' She added carefully, 'Before things get serious.'

Mademoiselle's eyes glittered with malice. 'You mean before they send for the police? You are a fool. They will not do so.' She shrugged almost gleefully. 'Bertrand knows what I am truly owed, and he can afford the loss. Nor will he want the *brouhaha* of an action in the courts. The Duchard name is a proud one and your sister's disgraceful *affaire* is scandal enough for the moment.'

She nodded. *'En plus,* I have been clever, taken care *a couvrir ma marche.* They will be glad just to let me go.'

'You say you love Monsieur Bertrand,' Ginny whispered. 'Yet you can do this to him.'

Monique Chaloux gave a contemptuous laugh. 'Love? What do you know of love, a silly girl with water in her veins instead of blood? No wonder Monsieur Andre amuses himself elsewhere. You deserve no more.'

She reached for a large leather bag on the floor beside her, stuffing the remaining statements into it. *'Et maintenant,* I am finished here,' she added.

'But I'm not.' Ginny lifted her chin. 'Because

you're not getting away with this. I'm going straight to Monsieur Bertrand.'

She turned and went quickly down the stairs. As she reached the turn, she was pushed violently as Monique barged past her. She grabbed desperately at the rail of knotted silk rope on the wall, missed and fell forward, crying out as her body rolled and jolted down the remaining stone steps, crashing into the door at the bottom.

She felt a sudden blinding pain in her head, and the world went dark.

There was something shining above her, a light so bright it managed somehow to penetrate her closed eyelids, making the previous darkness seem friendly. She tried to ask someone to switch it off, but her voice wasn't working.

Also somewhere in the distance, someone else was speaking. Whispering, so that she had to strain to hear him, 'Virginie, *mon ange, mon amour.* Wake up, *chérie.* Look at me, *je t'en supplie.'*

The voice was familiar but the words made no sense. No sense at all. Just the same, she tried to obey, but forcing her eyes to open was altogether too much of a struggle. Besides, she was aware of pain, a ferocious ache like the jaws of an angry animal waiting to devour her.

It was easier to decide that she must be asleep and dreaming, and let herself slide back into the tenuous comfort of her inner night-time.

But the voice would not let her rest, calling her, '*Ma douce, ma belle.*' Commanding her, '*Reveille-toi.*'

And he was being joined by others, none of whom she recognised except for Cilla, sounding strangely choked, as she begged, 'Oh Ginny, please speak to me. Please say you're all right.'

And she wanted to say crossly, Of course I'm not all right, because the pain was no longer at bay, but all around her, grinding at her when she attempted the simplest movement.

When, at last, she opened her unwilling eyes, she discovered a different kind of light in the form of the sun streaming through a large square window, in a room with ice-blue walls where she lay in a high, narrow bed.

And she thought—Where am I? What's happened to me?

She turned her throbbing head slowly, wincing, and saw Andre, unshaven, dishevelled and fast asleep in a chair a few feet away.

He looked terrible, she thought, filling her eyes and her heart with him, physical discomfort almost forgotten as she thought of his voice—the things he'd said to her. Until, of course, she also remembered it had only been a dream.

She said his name, her own voice a husky shadow of itself, but somehow he must have heard it because his eyes snapped open and he sat up. For a heartbeat he stared at her with something like incredulity, then, with a noise like a yelp, he was out of the chair and racing to the door, yelling, 'Philippe.'

Within seconds, the room was full of people led by a thin dark man with lively dark eyes and a goatee beard, who shone something like a pocket torch but infinitely more powerful into both her eyes and took her blood pressure before asking her in careful English if she knew what day it was.

It took a moment, but she told him.

'You know why you are here?' the doctor enquired. 'What happened to you?'

For a moment Ginny was silent, then as if a curtain in her mind was slowly being raised, she remembered being jostled. Trying to save herself but pitching forward.

She croaked, 'I fell. On some stairs.'

He nodded approvingly. '*Très bien. Vous êtes couverte de bleus, mademoiselle, mais rien est cassé. Vous comprenez?*'

'I'm very bruised but nothing's broken,' she said obediently. Then tensed, smothering a gasp of pain. She whispered, 'But the baby. I've lost my baby, haven't I?'

'*Heureusement, non.*' He smiled at her reassuringly. 'As I told Andre, a fall does not always lead to *une fausse couche,* and the child is still safe and warm inside you.

'No, our concern has been the blow to your head which has caused *une commotion cerebrale.* A concussion.' He nodded. 'We shall carry out some more tests, but there is no internal bleeding and I believe the injury to be not serious.'

But there had been a serious injury of a very different kind, thought Ginny, as events and images began crowding back into her mind. And the results could be dire.

She said urgently, 'Andre—I have to speak to him. There is something he must know. *Quelquechose très importante.*'

He clicked his tongue reprovingly. 'It is more important that you rest and recover, *mademoiselle.* But,' he added, his face softening, 'I will allow you a few moments with your *fiancé,* if first you must take the painkiller and the sedative the nurse will give you, so that you sleep when he has gone.'

And how many tons of the stuff would it take to knock her out at nights when he'd gone for ever? she asked herself wretchedly as she swallowed the proffered pills.

When Andre came in, he looked as if he was wired to snapping point. Maybe his doctor friend should prescribe a sedative for him, thought Ginny, her heart turning over as he brought the chair close to the bed and sat.

He said, stammering a little, 'Philippe said—that you have asked for me. That you have something to tell me.'

His hand went out as if seeking hers, and she withdrew it quickly, knowing that his lightest touch, especially if offered only in compassion, could cause her more pain than any bruise.

She said breathlessly, staring down at the white coverlet, 'It's Monique Chaloux. I found her in the office shredding bank statements. She's been stealing money from you—probably quite a lot. I—I was coming to tell you about it when I—fell.'

There was an odd silence, and when she ventured to look at him, she saw that he was white beneath his tan, his eyes bleak with shock, and a kind of desperate disappointment.

Small wonder, she thought. After all, it was the last thing you wanted to hear about someone you'd known and trusted for so long.

At last, he said quietly, 'I think you mean when you were pushed. Monique has admitted to that too.'

'Admitted?' she echoed.

'Why, yes,' he said. 'At this moment, she is, as you would say, helping the police with their enquiries.'

'But you mustn't let her!' Ginny tried to sit up and wished she hadn't. 'She's going to say foul things in court about Cilla.' She looked away, swallowing. 'About her getting married. It will be dreadful—for everyone.'

He shrugged. 'Monique *est terriblement* snob, as all the world will tell you. And if Papa welcomes the marriage, as he does, what else can matter?'

She said in a low voice, 'Of course, you're quite right.' And paused, taking determined control of her emotions. 'How did you find out about Monique?'

'Jean Labordier from Credit Regional notified us that a new account had been opened in the name of the Domaine, and he wished to check the letter of authorisation. This, of course, was false,' he added with a grimace. 'But we arranged for the account to be left open to see what would happen. We discovered that Monique was quitting her *appartement,* so Papa tried several times to talk to her—almost to warn her, but it was of no use.'

'But how could she do this to your father, when she claimed to love him?'

'Because her love was not returned,' he said with sudden harshness. 'And she never learned to understand how that can happen—or to forgive.'

She said haltingly, 'That's—not an easy lesson.'

'I do not need to be told that.' Andre paused. 'Yesterday, Jean telephoned to say that one hundred thousand euros had been transferred to the new account. This morning she was arrested, with attempted murder added to the charges against her.'

Ginny gasped. 'Isn't that going much too far?'

'You think so?' he demanded roughly. 'When you could have fractured your skull—broken your neck? Do you know the agonies I suffered when you did not immediately regain consciousness? When I realised that Philippe was trying to warn me that because of the blow to your head, you could be brain damaged or suffer a fatal haemorrhage?'

He added, his voice shaking, 'And you could have lost our child.'

Yes, she thought. It could have happened. My one precious link to you taken from me. Leaving me with less than nothing.

She braced herself. Kept her tone spuriously bright. 'Yet here I am, safe and soon to be well again. Well enough to leave, anyway, and let you get on with your life.'

'A thousand thanks,' he said with intense bitterness. 'And now, unlike Monique, I suppose I must learn to forgive you. Even to hope you will find the happiness that I have been denied. All that I dreamed, if I was patient, I would discover with you, the love of my heart.'

In spite of her bruises, Ginny sat upright. 'You dare to say that to me?' Her voice was incredulous. 'To speak as if I am to blame for ending our mockery of an engagement? When you're planning to marry my sister?'

The dark brows snapped together. 'I—marry Lucille? What madness is this?'

'Oh, don't pretend,' she said hotly. 'You slept with her in England, and when she turned up here, you resumed the affair. Do you deny you encouraged her to stay for as long as she wanted?'

'No,' he said. 'That at least is true. But for Jules' sake, not mine. I could see that he too had suffered the *coup de foudre*—that moment when you look into a woman's eyes, and know that your life has changed for ever. He begged me to persuade her, and against my better judgement, I did so.'

'Jules,' Ginny repeated. 'You mean—Jules Rameau?'

'How many others do you know?' Andre demanded impatiently.

She said slowly and carefully, 'You're telling me that Cilla and Jules are together and planning to be married?'

'Yes,' he said. *'C'est incroyable, n'est-ce pas,* what love can do?'

'Well, yes,' Ginny said doubtfully.

'You do not see them as a couple? Yet Jules is the strong man that I knew she truly needed. With him, she has grown into a woman, not the spoilt, selfish child who came to my hotel room because she was bored with her fiancé, and wanted a little adventure.'

Ginny gasped. 'Did she tell you so?'

'Of course,' Andre said drily. 'And she was most

shocked when I made it equally clear that she was wasting her time and sent her away.'

'But she let me think you'd been lovers.'

'She is no longer that person, Virginie. Ask her again and she will tell you the truth.' He paused. 'But when she arrived here, it was that capacity for making mischief that concerned me when she and Jules began spending time together.

'I was not really sure of her true feelings until our day in Beaune. I needed to find out if she was truly committed to spending her life here in Burgundy, or whether she would decide in the end that England had more to offer.

'Because Jules, I know, will never leave here.' He added sombrely, 'And I could not bear for her to break his heart, Virginie, as you were breaking mine.'

'But you only brought me here because you realised I might be pregnant and you felt guilty.'

'Yes, there was some guilt,' Andre admitted. 'Because I had rushed you into a relationship you were not ready for. But I always intended to bring you back here with me, *ma mie,* because I was very aware I could not live without you.'

He paused. 'When I came to the house for the reading of the will, I was late, I was tired and I was angry because I knew the problems it would cause. Then the door opened, and you were there, with my father's dog at your side, as if you were waiting for me. I saw how pale you were, how unhappy, and I wanted to pick you up in my arms and keep you safe for ever.

'And in that moment, I knew that the greatest happiness this life could bestow would be to come home each day and find you waiting for me.'

She said unevenly, 'But you were still angry.'

'That is true.' He was rueful. 'Because it was something I did not expect and I do not appreciate shocks. Also, if I am honest, it was something I did not want. A wife—one day, *peut-être*, but not immediately. But you changed my mind, *ma belle.*'

She looked away, her face warming. 'But I'm not beautiful. Cilla's always been the pretty one.'

He said gently, 'Virginie, *chérie,* my sweet idiot, to me you have always been enchantment. And on the night of our engagement, in that black dress with the rubies at your throat, you were the essence of beauty.'

He shook his head. '*Mon Dieu,* I wanted you so badly, I was going crazy.'

'You asked me to sleep with you,' she mumbled.

'But then you never came near me. And you started sleeping down at La Petite Maison.'

He said wryly, 'Because I knew I could not trust myself. Clothilde had warned me that making love in the first months is not always good for the baby, and as our child seemed the only reason you were with me, I felt I could not take the risk. That I must stay away.'

He paused. 'And once you realised that Jonathan Welburn was a free man, you hardly allowed me to touch you. In fact, you shrank from me, making me believe you still cared for him.' He spread his hands almost despairingly. 'And, if you no longer wanted me, how could I keep you tied here in a marriage without love or even a little human warmth?'

He sighed. 'Papa had told me how he struggled with the knowledge that my mother had not married him for love, although she grew to care deeply for him. But that might not have happened, and he did not want me to suffer in the same way.'

'I thought you belonged to my sister,' Ginny whispered. 'That she was taking over—replacing me. I thought if I distanced myself from you, it might not hurt so much. Instead, it was a thousand times worse.'

He groaned. 'Forgive me, *ma belle*. I wished only for you to rest more, at least until you stopped being sick, and for Lucille to be of some use and help you. Clothilde told me you are not as strong as she could wish.'

Ginny lips curved slowly into a smile. 'Well, the baby and I have survived a tumble down the stairs, so perhaps we're not as fragile as you think.'

She stretched out her hand, and he took it in his, holding it for a long moment as if it was something infinitely delicate, infinitely precious before raising it gently to his mouth. Then turning it, he let his lips and tongue softly and sensuously caress her palm, and kiss the length of each slender finger, suckling their pointed tips.

He must have felt her voluptuous shiver of delight, because he raised his head and smiled back at her, his eyes alive with passionate tenderness.

'So, when your bruises are healed, shall we put the matter to the test—on our honeymoon, *peut-être*?'

'Now I have a condition,' she said and saw his brows lift. 'I want you to drop any charge of harming me against Monique Chaloux,' she went on quickly. 'I'm not prepared to add to her troubles.'

Not, she thought, when I've known for myself all the terrible pain of jealousy and unrequited love.

'You ask for that?' Andre shook his head. '*Mon Dieu,* Virginie, when I saw you lying there, I thought I had lost you.'

'Instead, you've found me,' she said softly. 'We've found each other, perhaps thanks to her.'

There was a pause then he sighed. '*Soit.* Let it be as you wish.'

Suddenly Ginny realised she was smothering a yawn. 'Oh, no.' She gave a little wail of dismay. 'I let them give me a sleeping pill.'

'Sleep then.' Andre was still holding her hand, clasping it in both his own, his gaze warming her. 'Dream of me, *mon ange,* and when you wake, I will still be here beside you.'

'You promise?' She was beginning to drift.

'*Pour le restant de nos jours,*' he whispered as her eyes closed. 'For as long as we both live.'

* * * * *

439